A *Family* BY
CHRISTMAS
LITTLE SHOPS ON HEART STREET

A *Family* BY CHRISTMAS

LITTLE SHOPS ON HEART STREET

VIV ROYCE

Entangled Publishing, LLC
2614 South Timberline Road
Suite 105, PMB 159
Fort Collins, CO 80525
rights@entangledpublishing.com

Bliss is an imprint of Entangled Publishing, LLC.

Edited by Candace Havens
Cover design by Bree Archer
Cover photography by Todor Tsvetkov, Weedezign, and StockPhotosArt/Getty Images

Manufactured in the United States of America

First Edition October 2019

Bliss
An Entangled Imprint

Chapter One

Snipping the mini marshmallows in halves with her scissors had been a brilliant idea, as they were now the exact right size for the edge of her miniature chocolate mug, but putting them onto a narrow edge with tweezers was rather a tough job.

Emma Miller exhaled in frustration as another little bit of fluffy pink shot in an unwanted direction and, after a bounce on her work counter, even jumped over the edge to the floor. If she kept going like this, she'd be knee-deep in marshmallows before her twenty mini mugs for a new customer were done.

The advice given on a business seminar she had taken echoed in her mind. *"Time invested has to be earned back by income derived from the activity."* Well, her time invested here would certainly not be earned back. Nevertheless, doing this made her incredibly happy.

Sometimes she still didn't believe it. That she had managed to rent a building on coveted Heart Street where all the artisan, often family-owned shops were. She was a stranger to town, an outsider, whom people might have blamed for muscling in on their territory. But everyone had been kind and welcoming.

Emma glanced through the open door of her workspace into her shop where a small imitation Christmas tree sat perched on the counter, decorated with miniature golden balls and fake snow. A present from all business owners to celebrate her first three months on Heart Street. With Christmas on the calendar in just two weeks' time, her order list was full, and every minute put into making more sweet treats to deliver to customers in the run-up to the holidays.

What was that? Something seemed to move behind the glass counter. It stirred there, red and black.

Emma angled her head to look better. The bell over her door hadn't jangled, but then again, she wasn't 100 percent sure that she would have heard. She'd been too busy telling those pesky little marshmallow snippets to stick. *It can hardly be a customer unless they're crouching on hands and feet.*

Putting her tweezers down on a plate by her side, Emma straightened up and walked through the open door in the shop's space. Through the display case the shape took on a more solid form. And as she halted and leaned down over the counter, it fully materialized into a snow-drizzled little girl. The flakes rested tenderly on her black hair, which hung in long curls down her narrow shoulders. The cute red coat she wore was snow splattered as well and her feet, sticking in red boots, were moving as if she wriggled her toes to get the December cold out.

Big blue eyes gazed earnestly into hers. "I stood outside a little," the girl said in a chirpy, nervous tone. "To think it over. But I have to do it, you know. I have to."

She moved her feet again, maybe not to dispel the cold but her apparent nerves.

Emma had no idea why her shop or her person would be

intimidating to a little girl, but nevertheless put on an even more welcoming smile. "You could have come in right away," she said. "You can have a look around if you want to. You don't need to buy anything."

The leader of the business seminar would cringe, as he had drilled into them that every opportunity for a sale should be taken. But Emma didn't particularly care for taking money off little girls who probably didn't have all that much on them anyway. She remembered her own days of being seven, or eight, like this little one, and pushing her nose against shop windows to gaze inside and dream of everything on offer. In a house full of foster children there hadn't always been the financial means to give presents. Birthdays and Christmas had been made special by handcrafted gifts and lovingly handwritten postcards, but still Emma had sometimes just longed for the talking doll or the puppy on a leash you could walk.

She smiled even wider. "Is there anything here you really like? I could, uh…" She glanced around as if to see that no one overheard them. "Let you try some."

"Oh, no." The girl's cheeks turned as red as her little coat. "I don't want any. It's for Daddy."

"For your father?" Emma asked, a little surprised. Her customers were mainly women who bought the treats for other women—mothers in law, sisters, friends—or who wanted to impress guests at a party.

The girl said, "You have to make them especially. Grandma said it. She said that you can make people fall in love."

Emma's eyes widened. "That I can do what?" she asked.

The girl hung her head and said something in a whisper.

Emma rounded the counter and squatted beside the girl. "What's that? You can say it in my ear." She tucked the white cotton of the protective cap behind her ear as if to hear better.

"What's that for?" the little girl asked, eyeing the cloth on Emma's head.

"It's for when I work with the chocolate. To prevent any hairs from falling into it. That wouldn't be nice for the customers. I also wear plastic gloves when I take bonbons out of their tray and put them into a box. So I don't leave any fingerprints on them."

The girl giggled. "You're smart." She looked Emma over. "I think you can really make people fall in love."

"Why did your grandmother say that?"

"I don't know. But it was about chocolate. And you have a chocolate shop here. You can help me to…" She fell silent and eyed Emma as if she was suddenly reluctant to share. She wore a mitten and, turning her palm up, she opened her hand. On the wool rested a few coins, probably not making two dollars. "I don't know if you sell them like Grandpa sells plants," the girl said with a weighty frown. "They go one by one or by the dozen. I'd really like a dozen, because then I can be sure Daddy will really fall in love. You see, I don't think he wants to."

"I see," Emma said, furiously trying to process everything.

"Last week Aunt Fay was watching a movie where they kiss, and she asked Daddy to come and watch with her. But he said he didn't want to see it. And when he noticed I had overheard, he told me that he doesn't like kissing. That he thinks it's stupid." She laughed. "He asked me if I think it's stupid too and he tickled me all of the time. I had to laugh and laugh until I fell on the floor. Then he carried me to bed." She became serious again. "Then I thought about kissing. I don't know if it's stupid. Grandma and Grandpa kiss all the time and they're happy. I want Daddy to be happy." She put her mitten on Emma's arm. "Please help me make Daddy happy again."

Emma's heart clenched at the tone of the little girl's voice.

She had to clear her throat before she could say, "But I don't really understand what I should do. What's your name?"

"Casey. Casey Galloway."

Of course. Now the reference the girl had made to plants clicked into place. Galloway Nursery was well known in the entire region. They delivered plants and trees, mostly Christmas trees at this time of year. So, the elderly man Emma had seen around town with his white beard, as if he was Santa himself, and with a matching deep belly laugh was this little girl's grandfather.

It must be great to have a big extended family and get together for Christmas.

"So, you're staying here for the holidays?" she asked.

Casey shook her head. "It's not holidays yet," she corrected with a serious expression. "Miss Evelyn has made us a calendar in the classroom. And we cross off the days we still have to go to school. Miss Evelyn is really fun. I was worried first when we came here that I wouldn't like school. But I do."

"Do you live here?"

"Yes, for..." Casey thought long and hard, her face scrunched up in concentration. "Fourteen months now." She beamed that she had worked it out. "That's more than a year. That's a long time, right?"

"A very long time. I've only been here for three months."

"It's good you came. You can help me now." Casey presented Emma with the money again. "Is this enough?"

"What exactly do you want?"

"A dozen chocolates to make Daddy fall in love with Miss Evelyn."

Emma almost lost her balance and had to put a hand to the tiled floor to stay seated on her haunches.

"If a dozen is too much," Casey said quickly, "ten is okay as well, I guess. But he will have to eat some for a few days.

Things don't work when you don't try them for a few days. That's what Grandma told Grandpa when he had a cough and he wouldn't take any more honey because it's so sweet. Grandpa doesn't like sweet things, but Daddy does. He always pinches Aunt Fay's chocolate cake. I saw him do it once and he told me not to tell. You will keep it a secret, won't you?"

"Of course," Emma reassured her at once. Her legs had turned numb from sitting in this awkward position. She straightened up again and leaned down to Casey. "I think I don't need any money for this special assignment. It will be a Christmas gift. Just tell me what flavors your daddy likes best."

"Chocolate," Casey said with a nod.

Emma laughed. "But I make all kinds of chocolate. Extra dark and white and cream. With fillings."

"You have to decide. You know what to make. You are the…" Casey thought deep again. "Expert. Grandpa says you must never argue with an expert."

Emma had rarely taken such a delicate order, phrased in such vague terms, but she couldn't say no to this cute little girl. Casey obviously had a big loving family here in Wood Creek to look after her, but still she wanted one thing: to make Daddy happy.

Emma's gut clenched. *She came to the wrong person*, a pestering voice in her head whispered. *In all of Wood Creek you must be the only one who knows nothing about happiness. About falling in love. You can't do this. Tell her your schedule is full, because of Christmas.*

She bit her lip. But looking at the bonbons in her counter, her chest widened, and she pulled back her shoulders. *I can make chocolate. I can shape it and fill it with the most delicious flavors. I do know about that, and that's exactly what Casey's here for. I can help her.*

And I will.

Her head whirled with ideas and her hands itched to get started. Even if she had to work deep into the night to find the perfect combinations, she would. This assignment was special. Emma winked at Casey. "I'll get your order ready for you. You can pick up the first batch tomorrow. Then you can give them to your father over the weekend. I'll have new ones ready on Monday."

"Do you think it will work?" Casey asked eagerly. Her eyes shone with a bright confidence that fanned the ideas drifting through Emma's mind. *Salted caramel. Cream with strawberries. Rum and raisin.*

"Of course it will work," she said.

Oh, really?

What if Casey's dad falls in love with Miss Evelyn and she turns out to be engaged or something. You don't know a thing about that teacher. You're just throwing yourself into this, but you're not a kid anymore. You should know better.

She added quickly, "I'm sure that when you wish for your father to be happy again, it will come true somehow."

Casey exhaled in relief. "I knew it. Thank you." She ran to the door and opened it, again without ringing the bell above. She slipped out into the snow that was falling even denser. Emma followed her to the door and watched her as she halted to look left and right before crossing and vanishing from sight behind a parked van. As her little form was no longer there to discern through the snowy curtain, it almost seemed unreal, as if the whole encounter hadn't happened. Couldn't have.

The chilly wind breathed across Emma's face, and she shivered, ducking back inside. Her foot slipped, her weight tilted to the side and her arm swung up to keep her on her feet. Her heart pounded, and she sucked in a breath. The tiles underneath her feet were wet with a thin layer of dirty water.

Melting snow.

Casey has been here. It's all real. A real assignment, and a huge responsibility.

So maybe Casey's dad didn't want to fall in love, and maybe Miss Evelyn was engaged to another, but that wasn't the point. The point was doing what Casey had asked. Reassure her she had done everything in her power for her daddy's happiness.

Emma nodded to herself and retreated into her workspace, where the marshmallows were still waiting for her. Picking up the tweezers, her thoughts were circling on her delicate assignment.

What to make for this man who had proclaimed to hate kissing…

Chapter Two

"Coffee?"

Grant Galloway froze on the top step of the stairs, his hand on the railing, as if he was caught red-handed sneaking in after staying out too late.

"Sure, Mom," he called back down in as casual a tone as he could. Good thing he now knew she'd be coming up to the workroom to bring him the coffee as soon as she had finished making it fresh. She knew that once he was caught up in work, he forgot everything around him, including her delicious mocha. Tonight, however, Grant wasn't going to work on administration or new orders for trees but an incredibly exhilarating, even forbidden thing.

On the door of his workroom was a big piece of paper with crooked lettering in bright red reading *husssssh, Daddy is working.* Casey had made it after he had explained to her that this was his office now, and he couldn't read her stories while it was office time. The strokes of each letter had been scratched into the paper with energy, and he bet she had been at it with the tip of her tongue between her lips. Anything to help him out. *That's my little princess.*

She had no idea he had used the so-called office to hide in when he just couldn't deal with her rushing in and chirping about some storybook to him, demanding he come and read to her. In her bedroom, with the warm light on and her looking up at him with her teddies and stuffed elephants and little lions all tucked in around her, his throat had been too tight to get out a "once upon a time." A little princess, left alone, no mother anymore to care for her. He'd rather work hard for hours on end, closing the workroom door as a barrier, and let Grandma read Casey stories—when he just couldn't do it without crying. Without making Casey cry as well. *Anything to keep the pain away from you, princess.*

Grant reached out a finger and touched the words with a smile. They had made a special deal that when he didn't come in at night for story time, he made it up to her in the daytime when they could run around the tree nursery and play hide and seek. It was easier when the sun was bright in the sky, easier to chase her and catch her and lift her high and laugh and not think of what they had been when there had still been three of them. Not just two.

Then "two" had meant "one short," but these days two made up his unit, his team. *The best team in the world, going to fly out on new adventures.*

Sitting down at the overloaded desk with the old computer, he logged onto his own account in which he usually worked on the administration and opened the email program.

No new emails.

No replies to his recent applications for jobs as a pilot. Silence. He hadn't put the emails through to his cell phone for that exact reason: the moment of backlash when there was no mail. A sort of deafening silence, whispering to him he was too old, and he'd never get back in.

Nothing a little persistence can't fix. He leaned forward

to click open the browser and surf to sites where he might find new job offerings, companies or individuals looking for an experienced pilot. For himself, he wasn't picky and would have taken on anything as long as it could get him up in the air again, but for Casey's sake there had to be some conditions met. He had to be able to work hours while she was in school. No more long international flights like he had done before. Only regional flights and only during daytime hours.

Which excludes just about everything on this list.

His shoulders were tight from leaning in, and he rolled them back, taking a few deep breaths. *The perfect vacancy is around somewhere. You just have to find it.*

"Break time." The door swung open wide, and his mother came in with the coffee, carrying a bright orange mug in one hand, a plate of cookies in the other. He minimized the screen quickly so she couldn't see what he was doing.

His heart beat fast like it had when he had come from school with a bad grade hoping she wouldn't ask how the test had been. Lying to her was no use as she always saw right through him. And he didn't want to lie, just keep his job search away from her a little longer. He wasn't sure he would actually find something and…she wouldn't be happy to see him leave. See *them* leave. She loved having Casey around.

"Walnut cookies." She put the plate close to him, the mug a little farther away so it couldn't get knocked over and ruin the keyboard. "Made them fresh this afternoon."

He already knew that, but he still widened his eyes as if their appearance was a total surprise. "Great." He inhaled their spicy scent. She had thrown in more than just walnuts. "Thanks, Mom."

"And drink your coffee…"

"While it's hot, I know." He looked up at her and grimaced in mock disapproval.

She smiled down and squeezed his shoulder. He scanned

for a surreptitious glance at the monitor. Did she suspect he wasn't working on the tree farm administration?

He grabbed a cookie and bit into it. It was soft and buttery, the spices rolling across his tongue. "Great," he mumbled around the bite.

She nodded, determined as if she had come to a decision. "I'll tuck in Casey." She hesitated a moment. "Don't work too late."

The door closed, and Grant let the breath he'd been holding go. No probing questions.

Not yet, anyway. Mom and Dad were gearing up for Christmas, the busiest time of the year for their tree farm. He didn't want to spoil the festive mood with the news he was thinking about leaving them.

He had said "temporary" of course, but that was months ago, and it was an easy thing to sort of forget.

Grant reached for the mug and wanted to take a swallow, but as the coffee hit his mouth, it was too hot still and he put it back where it had come from. A small box sat tucked away under some papers. It was bright red and he was certain he had never seen it before. The top was decorated with a golden bow. It was tied very neatly but still he believed he detected the work of little fingers there. *Casey.* A present for him, a secret. He ran his fingertips across the bow as a silly grin spread across his face. *I love you and I'm so proud of you.*

She was probably in her bedroom, bursting to know how long it would take him to spot it and come to her.

On it, princess. He picked up the box. It was quite heavy and something solid shifted inside it. He weighed it on his palm, frowning hard. This wasn't some creative effort of paper and glue, clay perhaps, but more like...

Bonbons?

No way. How would Casey know he liked bonbons?

Still he pulled at the neat bow and lifted the lid. Before

his eyes could tell him anything, his nose had already found the answer. *Chocolate, yes...*

He cradled the box in his hands and savored the sight. The most exquisite creations he had ever seen sat in tidy rows. One was extra dark chocolate with a bit of gold dust. The other was creamy chocolate with marshmallow bits on top. And yet another white chocolate with a ribbon of dark tied around it and a tiny frosted flower on top. He picked up the marshmallow one without even thinking and popped it into his mouth. As he bit into it, something liquid rolled across his tongue and he closed his eyes in bliss. Chocolate truffle filling.

The smooth sensation of the sweetness made him sink back in his chair and stretch his legs at leisure. This was perfection.

But... He sat up again, snapped his eyes open and eyed the box. *What is it doing here?* Bonbons of this quality came at a buck a piece and there were a dozen in the box. Casey could never afford to buy such a thing. His mother, the avid baker, wouldn't buy sweet treats, and Dad had never had a sweet tooth.

So, who had gifted him these delights? Fay? Would his practical, down-to-earth sister who didn't like to splash on unnecessary luxuries buy bonbons at that price?

Grant lifted the box and carefully studied all sides, even the bottom. But it had no name on it anywhere. Not from the mysterious sender or the shop where it might have been bought.

He popped the extra dark one into his mouth and turned away in his swivel chair, hmmm-ing at the richness of the flavors. This was a master chocolate maker. Someone special. Someone he would have expected to find in London, Paris or Sydney. Not in Wood Creek, New Hampshire.

Wait a sec. He shot upright in his chair. Could that be the clue he was looking for? His eyes narrowed as he pictured the scene. A newspaper article his mother had mentioned a while ago. She had held it up to show him, but he had pretended not to be interested. It had been in that local newspaper that arrived on Wednesdays.

Grant pushed himself out of the chair and went to the corner where a twined basket sagged under the weight of dozens of old *Wood Creek Weekly*s. Kneeling beside it, he started to dig through the issues. It had been back in… Well, at least a few weeks ago. An article about a new shop. Mom had mentioned it to Fay. A chocolate shop. He figured it sold factory made chocolate and charged people a fortune for it. Then it had slipped his mind again. But now he was super interested. Summer fair, late night concert with piano and trumpet, jamboree… *New Bonbon Shop Opens on Heart Street.*

Bingo!

He barely glanced at the article—his eyes glued on the accompanying full-color photograph. It showed a beaming brunette in her thirties, dressed in jeans and a sweater, holding out a box full of chocolates. It was red just like his and showed various bonbons created with the eye for detail he had detected. This was the maker he had just silently admired.

He studied her closer, her sparkling eyes, her smile that was a little too wide, as if she was excited but also incredibly nervous. The proud gesture with which she held out the box reminded him of Casey when she had made something and showed it off to everyone who wanted to see. The charm bracelet on her left wrist sported a tiny silver whisk underlining her love of sweet treats. Down to that little detail, this woman was completely different from the person he had pictured behind that new shop Mom had mentioned. He had thought of someone who wanted to make a quick buck off the trusting locals. But this was someone who put everything into her creations and her brand-new business.

She had made chocolate for him? But why? Casey could never afford this. Besides, how would she know this woman?

He scanned the article for the chocolate maker's name. Emma Miller. She had moved here recently and started the shop. She lived in the small apartment over it. On Heart Street.

Grant held up the article and looked the beaming woman straight in the eye. "Well, Emma Miller of Heart Street," he said softly, "I'm going to look you up. To tell you that you make the best chocolate in the world. And to ask you how on earth that chocolate ended up on the desk in my workroom."

. . .

"I'm really not satisfied with this," the woman's sharp voice hissed down the line.

Emma clenched the receiver. "I'm sorry, but you did order dark chocolate. The taste is heavier than …"

"I know how I like my chocolate and yours just wasn't up to par. I want my money back. All my friends said the same. My tea party was completely ruined."

Emma took a deep breath. She had spent two evenings working on the bonbons for said tea party and giving the customer her money back would mean a dent in her budget for this week. *But it seems like diplomacy can't solve this and your reputation is worth more than your budget.* "I'll stop by later today to return the money to you. I'm sorry you had this experience."

The woman didn't even bother to say goodbye but disconnected.

Emma listened to the disheartening hum of a dead line and then lowered the receiver. It was unfair as the customer had herself ordered dark chocolate and with fillings that underlined that bittersweet tang. People who loved it clamored for more, but apparently the party guests had all been more the creamy chocolate type. Nevertheless, it had been the customer's explicit order and when taking it, she had had no reason to doubt the woman's judgment or inquire if she knew what she was doing.

Emma even bet, judging by the woman's attitude during the complaint call, that if she had asked, she would have been told off about it.

The shop bell jangled, and Emma rolled back her stiff shoulders to shake the unhappy feeling. Forcing a smile, she walked into the shop. On the other side of the counter a man stood, tall, dark-haired and broad-shouldered, in a woolen overcoat lightly dusted with snow. Flakes also hung in his eyebrows over eyes the deep brown of melting chocolate. His assessing look and hesitant smile gave her a moment's pause. *Seems he isn't here just to buy chocolate.*

"May I help you?" Her voice was a little unsteady. The angry customer's complaints still echoed in her head. She rubbed her palms together to regain her calm.

"I hope you can. I'm faced with a mystery you might be able to solve." He had a mellow, warm voice, and his smile deepened.

Emma found herself smiling in return even though his words didn't seem to make sense. "Me? Solve a mystery?"

"Yes. The mystery of the anonymous chocolate box." He dug his hand into the woolen coat pocket and produced a red box from her shop. "I can't show you the contents anymore. That's all gone." There was a mischievous twinkle in his eyes.

Chapter Three

Is he here to complain as well? Emma swallowed. Was he angry that she had made the chocolates without him knowing about it?

"This is one of your boxes, isn't it?" he pressed.

"Yes." *And I can guess who you are. Casey's father.*

"When I discovered them and tried one, I knew at once they didn't come from a supermarket and I remembered my mother mentioning a new shop in town. I found the article in the *Wood Creek Weekly.*"

Emma flushed. *Not that photo.* She still hadn't decided whether it was any good. With the critical scrutiny of a casual observer she had concluded her chignon was old-fashioned and her smile too wide, too eager to please. *Like a puppy who brings you a ball and drops it and waits, drooling and wagging his tail, to see if you're going to throw it for him.*

Those had been the words used to describe her presentation style during the business seminar she had attended. The participants had to evaluate each other's style, anonymously, so she had no idea who had written down those words about her. It wasn't bad to be compared to a puppy, she supposed—someone else had been compared to a shark—but on the other hand, it did make her feel immature and even uncapable of running her business. *Take that unhappy customer—you caved right away and agreed to give her the money back. That wasn't very businesslike.*

"I wondered," the man said, "how those chocolates ended up in my workroom. I suppose you didn't drop them off there."

"Oh, no, I've never been to the tree nursery. It does seem nice, but...I don't have the space upstairs for a large tree." Emma pointed up to where her apartment sat. The big sofa from her old place in Lansing filled out the entire living room space and in the tiny open kitchen every inch was covered in pans, mugs and cookbooks. "I gave the bonbons to your daughter."

"Gave?" His eyes surveyed her as if he wanted to read her innermost thoughts. "You use the best ingredients to create a top-notch product. Why would you give it away?"

"She did pay me. Sort of." Emma shuffled her feet. "She gave me what she had. It was a special order."

A smile tugged at the corners of his mouth. Still he continued in a stern tone, "I don't want my daughter to beg for favors. She knows she's cute and can get away with about anything." He reached into his other pocket. "Let me pay for the chocolate."

"No, that would spoil the whole point." Emma stepped forward, raising a hand to stop him from pulling out his wallet.

"What point?"

Emma took a deep breath. "Casey wanted you to have the bonbons." Could she really say to have him fall in love? *No way. I'd rather sink into the floorboards than tell him that.*

"It was a special assignment. She has a plan with it," she

concluded lamely.

He tilted his head, his eyes full of question marks. "A plan?"

Emma nodded. She didn't want to explain any further, as mentioning falling in love would be super awkward and weird.

"I offered to do the bonbons for the amount she could give me. It wasn't like she…forced me into it."

He held his head back and laughed, a booming laugh that filled her little shop with warmth and life. That twinkle was in his eyes again. "My daughter doesn't need to force people into things. She has her own methods. I don't know what she told you, but…"

"She told me," Emma blurted, "that she wants you to be happy again."

The mirth died down in his eyes and his facial muscles pulled tight.

"Happy?" he repeated as if he didn't understand the meaning of the word.

"Yes." *Great. This is really the way to handle it.* She could just kick herself but now that it was out, she had to push on. "Casey discovered you love chocolate." *And that you don't like kissing and she thinks chocolate can get you into kissing, and kissing Miss Evelyn, at that.*

No, that's terrible.

She said quickly, "She believes chocolate can make you happy again."

"Oh." He seemed to relax a bit. "Well, chocolate does make me happy and especially your chocolate. It's the best I've ever had."

Emma barely heard the compliment as she scolded herself for having chosen the easy way out. She couldn't leave it at this as he would certainly quiz his daughter about it and then hear the full story.

"Casey got the idea that chocolate can"—Emma cleared her throat before continuing—"make people fall in love and she wants you to fall in love with her teacher."

He stared at her. He opened his mouth as if he wanted to say something, then shut it again and stared some more. Emma's heart beat fast. Everything inside screamed: *turn away, fuss with something, fake a phone call, anything to get away from those eyes.* But she had let herself in for this, agreeing with Casey to do it, so she had to stand her ground now. *If only I knew what he was thinking. If he's mad or just puzzled.*

"And you encouraged that idea?" The words came out as if he were forcing them.

"She was covered in snow, cold and nervous and…I didn't want to disappoint her. I didn't say you'd fall in love because of the chocolate. I said that if she wanted you to be happy then surely something good would come out of it. That was no lie." Emma took a deep breath. "I couldn't tell her it doesn't work that way. She's just a little girl and she did it for you, really. Not for herself."

Again, there was hesitance in his features, darkness in his eyes as if he considered something hard. Then he said, "I know that she misses something. That I can't be to her what…" He fell silent and raked a hand through his hair. Snow drifted down from it onto his shoulders.

"I'm sure she loves you very much," Emma rushed to say. "And apparently Miss Evelyn helped her adjust in school. She just put one and one together."

A quick flash of tenderness sparked in his eyes. Then he sobered. "But you and I know it isn't that easy, don't we?"

"It's not like Miss Evelyn knows."

He scoffed. "I hope not. Contrary to what Casey seems to think, I have no intention at all to…get entangled with anyone. I'm just here for a while, you know. To get things back on track." He rolled back his shoulders as if he was tense. "Sooner or later we'll leave again. No attachments."

"I see. That makes sense."

He paced the shop and stopped at the wall with Christmas offerings, varying from small bonbon boxes to huge reindeer. All display material, to give the customer an idea of the offer. He said slowly, "It makes sense to you and to me, maybe, but obviously not to Casey. She does need..." He stood there as if he was searching for the right words among the chocolate Christmas trees dusted with powder snow.

"I'm sorry if I made this even harder. I just wanted to help her. I do understand that..." Emma bit her lip. *You don't understand. Casey is no orphan.* "I'm sorry."

He turned to her and smiled again. "I've got an idea. Why don't you help me make Casey's last Christmas here in Wood Creek extra special? I want her to have the best memories of it before we leave again."

"Me?"

"Yes, apparently she confided in you. She didn't tell anyone about coming here. That's not like her. She's usually pretty shy."

"But she likes Miss Evelyn. Why don't you ask her to..."

He came back to the counter with long strides, holding her gaze with his deep brown eyes. "Casey didn't go to her. She came to you. She somehow thought she could trust you and...that's huge. You see, Casey doesn't have a lot of people outside my family. I'd love for her to spend a bit more time with you and...make friends. She'll need to make new friends after we leave here and I'd love for her to work out how she can do that. She took the first step."

• • •

Indecision flashed in her eyes. Grant clutched the empty

chocolate box in his hand. *This is just coming out all wrong. Like she is some friendship tryout project. She already made the bonbons for a lower price than usual.*

"How about it?" He leaned forward. "You just said you haven't been to the tree nursery yet. Casey can show you around there. I'm sure we can even find a tree that fits into your apartment. We've got them that big…" He pointed to the ceiling. "And that small." He held his hand at the height of his hip. "We've also got loose evergreens, dried materials and candles to make a custom piece. You've made this all Christmassy…" He gestured around him at her red and golden decorations. "Let us bring a bit of Christmas to your home."

"That's a great offer. I'll be coming to the tree nursery anyway, for the Christmas fair. I have a booth there."

"Great. But that will be about *work* again." He wriggled his brows, and she began to laugh.

"Work is a big part of my life right now. I have so many orders to deliver. And the forecast for the next few days is really bad with lots of snow." Her expression turned worried as she glanced out her window as if to see if the skies were already unleashing a new load.

"Ah, but the tree farm has a snowmobile. If you want, I can help you with the deliveries. Faster, safer. You'll have some free time and could spend that with Casey. Personally, I don't know anyone I'd rather be with, but then I am her father."

Emma laughed again. It drove the hint of reserve from her features and opened them up like clouds breaking open under his plane and revealing a dazzling panorama.

She exhaled as if coming to a decision. "How could I say no?"

"That's a deal then. By the way, I'm Grant." He reached out his hand to her across the counter.

"Emma." She put her hand in his and shook with

surprising strength. "Welcome to my shop. I was making some salted caramel chocolate in the back. Want to try some?"

His mouth watered, and he nodded. "Would love to."

"I'll get it." She walked away quickly. She reminded him of a robin or a wren, a quick busy bird going about her business. Knowing exactly what she wanted. This space had been a real estate office before, he recalled, looking rather dark and uninviting. But her choice to paint the ceiling white created a sense of space. *Clever.*

She came back and handed him a large chunk of chocolate. He lifted it to his face and inhaled the amazing scent before even attempting a taste.

She smiled. "A real connoisseur."

He held the piece up as if toasting her. "To your shop. Must have been a big move, going to a new town and starting a business. Leaving behind what you used to know."

"I wasn't that attached to anything." It sounded rather vague and a bit evasive.

He studied her features closer as she rearranged something on the counter. Had heartache brought her here? A failed relationship? A loss?

The chocolate melted on his tongue in a combination of creaminess, caramel and a subtle hint of salt. "Perfect," he said. "Don't change a thing about it."

"It's so nice to have an opinion beforehand. You could become my taster."

"I didn't want to suggest it, myself."

He couldn't wait to see his daughter enjoying the Christmas season, ending their stay here on a high note, full of confidence they were ready to move into their new life together. That last step, finding trust again, that he could be a good dad and that Casey could make friends, build bonds with new people, adjust. It seemed closer than ever. With help from Emma, could everything fall into place?

Chapter Four

"Right. All set to go." Slightly breathless, Emma grabbed the two boxes with decorated chocolates off the counter and hurried into the shop front.

Grant turned to her. He wore a leather jacket with a shearling collar and dark jeans tucked into ankle boots. He grinned at her. "Ready to go?"

"Sure." Nerves fluttered in her stomach about the snowmobile. She had never ridden on one, but the offer of getting her deliveries around safely had been too good to resist. *Who knows, it might even be fun.*

"Let me hold those for you while you close up shop." Grant reached out to take the boxes from her hands. His warm skin brushed hers, and her breath caught. She struggled to find her key and lock the door. *Just nerves about this whole thing.*

"Done? This way." Grant went ahead of her with the boxes, at an easy pace as if he didn't mind the snow cluttering the pavement, frozen into deceptive icy heaps that could send her feet out from underneath her in a heartbeat.

"There we are." Grant halted beside something looking like a big motorcycle on skis. It had a box on the back to store things in. Grant clicked it open and placed the chocolates inside. "I normally use this for tools," he explained. "But I cleaned it before I came. Want to see if it meets with your approval?"

She inspected the inside. "Looks fairly clean to me."

"Fairly? Only just fairly, huh?" His brown eyes twinkled.

Say something funny.

Or just something.

Anything.

But her head was blank like the untouched snow on the roofs. Conversations in the store were usually practical, not needing rapid-fire witty retorts. *He was right, you work too much.*

"You have to wear a helmet. These things can go pretty fast and you want to be safe." He held out a red helmet dotted with white spots. "It's my sister Fay's."

Emma accepted the helmet and examined it doubtfully. "Do I take off my woolen hat then?"

"No, you catch a lot of wind on a thing like this." He reached out and pulled her hat deeper over her ears. "There, now put the helmet on over it. I don't want you to get cold. Do you have gloves?"

Emma stared at him, just conscious of the burn in her cheek where his hand had brushed her as he pulled her cap in place.

"Gloves?" Grant repeated, hitching a brow.

"Yes, of course. In my pocket. But first let me get this thing on." She put it on her head, feeling for the strap.

"Let me do it." Grant reached out and secured the strap, trying to move the helmet. His palm brushed her chin, and the warmth spread into her face and chest. The helmet didn't move, and he nodded in satisfaction. "There. Perfect."

Aftershave with pine notes swirled around her, and Emma quickly pulled the gloves out of her left pocket and fumbled to put them on, taking her time to pull them down well over her wrists.

Grant put on his own helmet, deep black emblazoned with golden wings on each side, and motioned to the snowmobile's broad seat. He gestured across it. "I'll sit in front because I have to steer, you hop on behind me. You have to hold on tight."

Emma stared at him. *Hold on? To him?*

I should have thought this through better. Her brain scrambled for a way out. There was none.

Grant smiled at her. "Don't worry, it's perfectly safe. I'll go slowly. For starters."

Thanks, that's very encouraging.

He swung his leg across the seat and sat down, looking over his shoulder at her. "Come on."

She rubbed her gloved hands together. She had an uneasy feeling the entire street might be watching.

But hey, Grant probably had all kinds of passengers. Miss Evelyn for instance? *Just a ride to get some chocolate delivered. Nothing personal.*

Emma clambered on behind him. Her balance was off, and she almost tipped to the other side, but once her foot found the railing it should rest on, she could prevent a landing in the snow.

Grant called over his shoulder, "Grab me tightly."

Uhm... Emma surveyed his back. *Grab him by the shoulders or the waist?*

She took a deep breath and reached out, putting her arms gingerly around his waist. The leather jacket creaked under her touch. The scent of it wafted in her face, mixed with the piney aftershave and the cold of the winter's day.

"Starting..." Grant called and turned the ignition on.

The snowmobile jumped forward, and Emma clutched his waist tighter. As a kid she had once made a pony ride where the animal had broken into an unexpected trot, pulling away from her older foster sister who had guided it. Emma had lived through a few terrifying minutes, clinging for dear life to the pony's neck before an adult had caught it and lifted her off. She had acquired a healthy fear of speed.

The growl of the engine tightened her stomach, and she struggled to breathe even. *Grant will be careful. He won't let me fall off.*

They glided along at a sedate pace, giving her a chance to glance at the other shops. No one paid any attention to them. An elderly lady with a poodle hurried into the welcome warmth of the bookstore. The homey feel of Heart Street wrapped itself around Emma, and she dared relax just a little bit.

• • •

The vicelike grip of Emma's arms around his waist loosened a fraction. *Good. This is supposed to be fun.* He'd give her time to get used to it, starting slow, then opening the gas step by step. Her hold would guide him. Tighten meant ease off.

He breathed the cold air full of the scent of snow and winter and had to suppress the urge to shout out loud. This was freedom. Not quite soaring above the clouds, but close enough.

He shook his head to get some pesky flakes away from his face. Behind him, Emma said something.

"What?" he called to her.

"The first delivery is to Court Street. Number forty-six."

Right. This is business. Not riding around on his motorcycle when he had been eighteen. For the fun of it, the feel of it, the sense of being all alone in the world. Everything was easy then, and under control.

Grant clenched the handlebars with a huff. His sense of control had been a lie. Oh, yes, on a bike, or in a plane, he could influence everything. Tell himself that he had planned the route, knew the safety protocols, had seen every airport before. He was the master of preparation; nothing took him by surprise. Nothing but that phone call. Telling him, while he sat on the bed in his hotel room in Tokyo, that Lily was dead. A heart attack. Gone. But that had to be a misunderstanding. Women of thirty-five didn't just die. Not out of the blue. She had never even mentioned feeling sick.

His mind had scrambled for a way out of the abyss that opened up around him, but his body had kept falling. There hadn't been a hold anywhere, just nothingness sucking him in, emptying him until he was part of the abyss. Dark, hollow.

Grant blinked against the sleet on his lashes, but really to block the unwanted memories of the hours spent on the edge of that bed, not knowing how he could ever stand up again. Walk. Fly back home and tell his daughter that her mommy was gone. That it was just the two of them from now on.

If he, an adult, didn't understand it, how could she? She was just a little girl.

A little girl, whom he barely knew. Oh, yes, he had played games with her and tucked her into bed at night when he was home. Between flights, and trips with friends. He brought her presents and he sang her songs when he was there. But sitting on that bed in Tokyo a voice had screamed in his head that it had never been enough, he hadn't been there for her, and he had done everything wrong, and now he was left, alone, to work it out with her.

Every accusation had been a punch in his gut, a blow drawing blood. No defense possible. No quick answers. No clever plans. Just one thought, welling up with the tears and burning its way across his cheeks: *even if I don't know how, even if I don't think I can, I have to do better. For her.*

Emma squeezed his shoulder. She called out, "Court Street was to the left just now."

"I'm—taking another route." *Snap to it.* Fortunately, he knew Wood Creek like the back of his hand. He could reach Court Street via Main and then back through Dougan.

"How are you doing?" he called to her.

"Fine. I kind of like this."

He chuckled. "Just kind of?"

· · ·

Emma held on tightly, blinking against the snow that kept on flying into her face and eyes like little needles stabbing her. The wind gushed into her neck and down her sleeves. She hunkered down behind Grant's back and was tempted to lean her head against him and close her eyes. *Focus on the delivery.* Mrs. Beaver had been rather demanding when she had been in the shop. She had wanted chocolates without filling, flat so she could present them on a silver tray, fifty in total, ten of each shape. But not plain chocolate, decorated with colors so as to bring pre-Christmas cheer to the ladies knitting group she was hosting tonight.

Emma swallowed hard. What if Mrs. Beaver didn't like what she had created? The recent customer complaint had knocked her confidence, and her heart beat fast as Grant turned the snowmobile into the drive of number forty-six. It had been freed of snow and the house itself was immaculate, with white lace curtains and small neatly cut bonsai trees in the windowsills. A wreath on the door in red and gold, everything tasteful and…perfect?

Emma took a steadying breath to silence the nerves churning inside. *The chocolates are exactly what she ordered.*

Yeah, that's what you thought last time.

Grant cut the engine, and she let go of him to clamber off.

"Do you want me to deliver them?" he asked.

Maybe Mrs. Beaver won't complain to him.

Stop it. "I've got it. Thanks." Her breathing was strained as she tried to move her legs, which had grown a bit numb in the cold.

Grant said, "Do you need help?"

"I'm okay." She managed to get her right leg across and stood leaning against the snowmobile, feeling a bit unsteady. She tried to wriggle her toes, but she could barely feel them.

Grant smiled at her and then hopped off easily. He rolled back his shoulders, his leather jacket creaking and sending another waft of aftershave her way. "Which of the boxes is it?"

"Top one." Emma struggled with the helmet's strap. She didn't want to ring the bell with a helmet on, like she was a pizza delivery boy.

Grant unlocked the storage in the back and handed her the box. The golden card tied on top wished Mrs. Beaver a merry Christmas.

"I'll hold your helmet," Grant offered.

Emma exchanged the helmet for the box and went to the front door of the house, pressing the bell with a nervous flutter in her stomach.

After what seemed like ages, the door opened. Mrs. Beaver surveyed her with a frown. Her face was flustered, and the apron she wore covered in flour. "Oh, yes, the chocolates. Put them in the living room for me, will you? I can't touch them now."

She stepped back to let Emma pass, directed her into the living room area and pointed at a low wooden table. A golden retriever came to sniff at Emma's boots, but Mrs. Beaver ordered him curtly to go back to his place. He glanced up at her with disbelief in his friendly face, but another command sent him trudging back to the corner where his basket stood.

Emma placed the box carefully on the table. She expected her to lift the lid and inspect the order, say something about how it had turned out, but she gestured to the front door. "I have tons left to do for the meeting tonight. Goodbye."

"Aren't you going to see if they are what..." Emma stammered.

"If I don't like them, I'll return them. If I like them, I'll pay my bill." Mrs. Beaver sounded final. "I heard that you gave a refund to someone else because the delivery was unsatisfactory. I'll pay when I'm satisfied."

Say you can't accept that, and you want her to look right now.

"I, uh..." Mrs. Beaver's flashing eyes made the words die on her tongue. "Yes, of course. I wish you a very merry Christmas."

Mrs. Beaver harrumphed as if she wanted to say bah humbug. She shepherded Emma out the front door and shut it behind her with a bang.

Emma cringed under the sound and walked back to the snowmobile with her shoulders pulled up. After the warmth inside, the air felt even colder and the wind breathing up her neck pushed goose bumps out on her arms. *You have to stand up for yourself. If you don't make money, you'll go bankrupt.*

"What's wrong?" Grant asked. "Didn't she like them? She closed the door on you like she was throwing you into the street."

That's exactly how I feel. Tears burned behind her eyes, but she forced a smile. "She's baking for the meeting tonight for which she also ordered the chocolates. She was just in a terrible rush, didn't have the time to pay me, either. But that will come, I'm sure. In a small town people are good for their word."

Grant looked her over and shook his head. "Taking

people on their word is good and fine, but you have a right to your money. She got her chocolates so you should have been paid."

"Yes, and then I'll have to refund when she doesn't like them. Now she didn't even want to check to see if she did like them, and then later she will complain that they weren't what she ordered." The words burst out in a furious rush. Emma bit her lip and looked down. Running the store alone, she never had a chance to complain about anything to anyone and let off steam.

The other shopkeepers were friendly enough, asking her how she was doing, but she didn't dare mention rude customers to them, for fear they would think her ungrateful or gossipy.

Grant leaned over. His eyes were concerned, searching her expression. "Don't you have some business rules that apply when people have a complaint? Fine print. It's amazing what you can do with it."

Emma had to smile in spite of her dejection. "I was told at the business seminar that I need some general terms and conditions, but…it's such a hassle to put it all together and I don't know if I could enforce them. How? Turn to an attorney? Or enforce payment via a third person? I can't see myself do it. I want to make friends here around town, not alienate people."

Grant sighed. "This sounds very familiar. My parents have had the tree farm here for all of their lives. That is, my dad grew up on it and then he went to college and met my mom and they came back together to take over when my grandparents retired. They know what it's like to run a business in a town where you know everyone.

"My mom is the worst. She's always giving people things for free. Because she knows they're on a tight budget, or it's for a good cause. Which is fine, but the tree farm supplies our income. Not just for my parents but also for my sister Fay and her husband. The same thing applies to you. You have to live off the chocolates, pay your rent, your bills."

"I do have some savings," Emma countered weakly.

Grant shook his head. "You sound like my mom. I've never had any luck with her, either." He said it in a light tone, but his eyes were serious.

Emma touched his arm a moment. "I do appreciate your advice. It's just that...I want people to like my shop. To love my creations."

To like me. To embrace me and welcome me here.

She averted her eyes. "I'm just bad at taking criticism."

"That goes for most of us." His voice sounded nearer as if he had leaned closer to her. "Don't change because of criticism, Emma. Your chocolates are something special. Anybody telling you anything different probably never had great chocolate like yours."

She looked up into his kind eyes. "Really?"

"Really, and you can trust my judgment. I've had chocolate all over the world. I know."

"All over the world?" What had a man who worked on a tree farm in New Hampshire been doing all over the world?

"I'm a pilot. I used to fly internationally. All the big cities. Paris, Vienna, Rome, Tokyo. Sydney, Moscow. The first thing I did was stalk the sweet shops. Bonbon shops if they had them." He smiled. "I can compare your creations to the best international offerings. And I can tell you I never had finer chocolate."

Emma should have been grateful for the compliment, felt proud she was in the same league as those working in big cities, catering to events and perhaps even royalty, but she was just stuck on that one word. "Pilot?" she repeated. "You don't work on the tree farm?"

"I did for a while, yes, but I'm going back to flying." He seemed to hesitate for a moment. "Mom and Dad don't know yet, but I'm looking for jobs."

Leaving. Leaving. The word that had haunted her all her life. People were always leaving. Or she was leaving. Leaving for the next foster family. Leaving for a new town to settle into. Shipped off again, moved around.

She shivered. It was so very cold around them. *Don't be silly. You knew. When Grant explained to you, in the shop, that he wasn't getting entangled with anyone, he mentioned that he wouldn't be staying here forever.*

And that's okay.

"Can we go to the next delivery?"

"Yes, of course. Here's your helmet. Hop on."

She secured the strap tightly and sat down behind him, even more reluctant to wrap her arms around his waist. It was so good to do this with someone else, experience a togetherness she normally had to do without. A bit of backup when she faced a tough situation, like a thumbs up "you're doing okay." She could get used to that. But Grant and his cute daughter weren't here to stay. Goodbye, yet again. *Make it easy on yourself. Don't get attached to them. Your new life is in Wood Creek.*

She'd drill that into her head until it became her first response as soon as she thought of him or his daughter, met with them, spent time with them. *Have fun while it lasts but don't get attached.*

Chapter Five

Grant's muscles tightened when Emma went to the door of the next house. He had hated to see her so pale and uncertain when she had come back from Mrs. Beaver. How could people treat her like that? She had worked hard on their chocolates, and they didn't even glance at them but already counted on a refund as if Emma hadn't put in the best ingredients, time, effort.

Anger mingled with his nerves and he kept his eyes on her as she stood at the door, waiting. Her back was straight, not showing any sign of worry. *Show them what you're made of.* He wished he had told her that, giving her a thumbs-up as she walked away, to make her smile.

But maybe it was weird to even think she needed that. She was used to fending for herself. She had built that business by herself.

The door opened, and an elderly lady waved her inside. The cold wind blew around Grant and he shifted his weight, rubbing his hands together. He checked his watch to see how long she'd been inside. His parents had always had each other to run their business, discussing a setback after dinner, when they believed the kids were in bed.

But Grant had sometimes sneaked down the stairs to listen in, wanting to help in some way. When his dad talked about difficult customers and plants that weren't quite right, his mom would put her arm around him and tell him it would be okay. They'd make it through, somehow—because they had each other.

Did Emma have someone to vent to, confide in? *You don't know anything about her.*

Emma came out again, her steps light, her face beaming. She rushed to him, waving something. It was a twenty-dollar bill. "She loved them and even gave me something extra because it's Christmas time."

He was so happy for her that he almost reached out his arms to hug her. *Hold it right there.*

He cleared his throat, putting his hands on his back. "That's great. Do you want to take a short spin outside of town? See *real* winter?" He winked at her.

Her forehead furrowed, and he was certain she'd say no. But then she smiled mischievously. "Let's go for it."

The compliments and the extra money had obviously boosted her mood, and she seemed ready to let go for a bit.

He sat down and waited for her arms to lock around his waist. "Hold on," he said and turned the ignition on. He made sure not to hit the gas too hard, as he didn't want her to be afraid. But he did want her to experience the rush of speed. The sense of being able to fly. Weightless. Free.

She clung to him but didn't tell him to stop. He steered the snowmobile out of town, onto a road that stretched between wide white fields. The sky above cleared, and a bleak winter sun shone down on them. It sparkled on the ice crystals formed on grass and tree branches, turning the landscape into a twinkling winter world created just for them to play in.

He opened the gas a bit more, and the snowmobile jumped forward. Grant whooped and laughed, holding his head back.

This was the life. Just him and the road—*and* Emma, behind him, experiencing this adventure with him.

"Stop," she called, and he hit the brakes. "What is it?"

"Just hold on for a sec." Emma clambered off. Her eyes were wide and sparkling, her cheeks red from the cold wind. "There's a snowman there. He's holding something in his hand, a rope. I'm going to make him a dog. Won't take long." She bounded off, light on her feet like a deer, jumping across heaps of snow, rushing into the field where the snowman stood. She crouched down, gathering handfuls of snow. In no time, she had created the body of a dog on low legs and then worked on the head.

A dachshund. Look at those ears, the perky snout. She's not just an artist with her chocolates.

"Let me try as well." A little away from her he worked on his own dog. He had built lots of snowmen with Casey and would grade his skills at an *A* for gathering snow, *B* for molding it, and *C* for making it actually look recognizable. *She'll never guess what breed this is.*

"Do you do this often?" he called to her. "Sneak away after work and donate snow dogs to snowmen?"

Emma laughed. "I wish. My life really centers on chocolate right now. Finding the right ingredients, trying new flavors. Oh, and I only finished painting my apartment last week. I haven't had any time off since I got here. Cleo keeps telling me I need to join a choir or book club or something to meet people and make friends, but honestly, at night I'm beat and don't want to go out."

"Cleo? Oh, Cleo Davis from the bookstore."

Emma nodded. "When I was redoing the shop, she helped me paint the ceiling. She also brought me lunch a couple of times just to make sure I ate something." She rolled her eyes. "Her words, not mine. And it wasn't that bad really. I'm just focused on getting everything set up and running. I can socialize later." She rose to her feet, her breathing ragged, studying the dachshund at her feet. "When I moved here, I had this idealistic idea of getting a dog and going out for long walks every day. My former apartment had a no pet policy, you know, and it seemed like something I could finally do. But I only want to go through with it when I have enough time to put into my new friend. Maybe in January, when all the Christmas madness is over." She turned to him. "What are you making?"

"Have a look. Can you guess?"

Emma came over, plowing through the deep snow. Her silence as she studied the object confirmed his fear.

"It's a large dog," she said at last. "Maybe a German shepherd?"

At least she figures it's a dog, not a polar bear. "It's supposed to be a husky." Grant grunted ruefully. "I guess my imagination outruns my molding skills."

"Let me give you a hand. If that's okay."

"Of course." He'd gladly switch trying to mold that pesky snow for watching her do it for him. The expression on her face as she worked with utter concentration, the devotion to the smallest details. She put her all into it.

"There." She stood back.

He stared at the pointy ears, the snout, the briskness of the head. The whole husky feel. "You're amazing." Her eyes were bright as stars. Her hat was covered in snow, as well as the hair escaping from it. Snowflakes melted on her cheeks. He wanted to brush them away.

But he just nodded at her and said, "Great job. But I bet you're cold. How about some hot chocolate on me?"

• • •

That was so much fun! And he called me amazing.

Emma's head was so light she could run for a mile just with the energy inside her. *Steady, girl. Calm down. Come back to earth.* "Yes. Hot chocolate sounds great. Thanks."

He reached out his hand to her. "Come on then."

She didn't take it, fussed with her gloves. He stuck his hand in his jacket pocket and strode to the snowmobile which sat glinting in the sunshine. Her heart pounded so hard she could barely draw breath. Grant Galloway was a dangerous man. He wasn't just a loving father to his little girl, but he was kind and attentive to her, caring for how her customers treated her. Taking her away from her busy schedule for a while. These moments here were exactly what she had needed to recharge, without even knowing that herself.

How had Grant known it?

It doesn't matter. Take it at face value. You had a good time.

Hot chocolate now, and then back to the shop to create more orders. After all, Christmas doesn't wait.

• • •

Emma's cheeks were warm from the cozy little cafe where they had drunk hot chocolate topped off with whipped cream and marshmallows. It had been great to see Grant enjoy the sweet treats, picking the marshmallows off one by one and popping them into his mouth.

Casey's right. Her sweets-loving daddy is very special.

She smiled at him as she reached for the keyring in her pocket to unlock her shop's door. "Thanks so much for your help. I have to get on the next batch of orders."

"Sure, let me know when they're due. I'll be driving

around town a lot the next few days getting trees to customers and I could take your chocolates along. Then you don't have to leave the shop."

"Good idea. If it's not too much trouble for you."

"Not at all. We can talk about it later today. How about I pick you up after closing hours? You can see the area at the tree farm where we'll be setting up the Christmas fair. Maybe you've got a few ideas about how to best decorate it. My parents have been running the fair for ages, and they stick to the tried-and-true elements everyone loves: music, lots of treats, and glitter. But they want to switch up the type of glitter every year." He winked. "A few outside ideas can't hurt."

Emma had no experience decorating for a large fair, and normally she would have said so, but now the sugar rush from the hot chocolate seemed to blur her brain a bit. *How hard can it be? Glitter and sparkle, like you did in your shop, just on a bigger scale.* "All right."

"Great." His smile widened. "See you later." He waved at her before opening the gas and roaring off.

She was about to slip the key in the lock when metal scraped against concrete, tightening her nerve ends. Next door, Cleo balanced precariously on top of a shaky ladder to change something about the colorful Christmas lights strung along the bookshop's front.

Looks like she needs a hand. Emma hurried over and grabbed the ladder to steady it for her. "Are you okay?" she called up.

Cleo Davis was the same age as her, with blonde hair pulled back in a sporty ponytail and outfits that usually had something to do with books. Today, it was a red jacket full of author names from Jane Austen to Robert Ludlum. Emma smiled when she recognized some of her own favorite authors—the Brontë sisters, Ellis Peters and Dorothy

Sayers—among them. With the chocolate shop, there was too little time for reading, but maybe she could catch up over the Christmas break.

Cleo glanced down. "Oh, thanks, Emma. One of the little lamps isn't screwed in tight and then the whole string of them doesn't work. I just have to check which one it is." Her hands moved rapidly from left to right, feeling the lamps one by one. "Ah. This one is a bit loose. Let's see if it's the culprit." She made a turning gesture. The lights came back on, throwing a cheerful glow across them. Pink, gold, blue, red.

"There you go." Cleo sighed in satisfaction and climbed down. "Done. I was worried I'd have to buy new ones. I don't have time. I'm busy wrapping some books for the Christmas fair raffle. All the shopkeepers are putting up prizes. But you probably know that. I saw you talking to Grant Galloway."

Heat crept up Emma's cheeks. Hopefully, they were already pink from the cold outside. "Yes, we were talking about the fair." She faltered, fidgeting with her gloves. "I heard it's a really big event the Galloways have been doing for ages."

Cleo nodded and whisked a lock of hair from her face. "A few years ago a council member wanted it transferred indoors, at the community center, and when word got out, there was a rush of calls to the mayor telling him nobody would be coming if it wasn't at Galloway's. The tree in which you can put your wish is theirs as well. Are you wishing for anything?"

"I don't know really. You?"

Cleo grimaced. "To keep my job."

"What?" Emma blinked. "How do you mean?"

She leaned over, lowering her voice. "My boss is close to retirement, and I don't know whether he will sell the shop to someone who wants to keep it as a bookstore or whether it will just close. In that case I'm out of a job. Nothing is certain yet, but the mere possibility kills the Christmas spirit for me. I mean, here I am, wrapping presents, while come January I could be closing the door one last time. I just can't believe it."

"Me neither." Emma's heart sank. The cute bookshop sitting empty? It pulled in lots of kids and brought a lively air to the whole street. "I thought you owned it. I always see you putting the displays outside and closing up at night. I didn't even know you had a boss."

Cleo smiled sadly. "He's older and doesn't spend much time at the shop these days." She studied the front with the colorful lights, the window full of books dressed up with fake snow and sparkly ornaments. "Feels like I'll never find another place quite like this. So much freedom to put my own spin on things. And if I can't find another job close by, I'll also have to move. I'll miss Wood Creek."

"I'll miss our chats. And we never got a chance to see that museum you mentioned to me. What was it? Wood crafting?" Why hadn't she made a little time for friendship instead of pouring it all into the shop? But if she had, she'd be losing yet another friend.

"I want to stay." Cleo held her gaze. "I would do anything to keep the shop open, but there's no way that I can buy it. I don't have enough savings. And the bank needs a business plan that proves it will be profitable. I just don't know if I could pull it off."

"You should at least give it a try. I mean, does your boss know you want to keep it open? Maybe he's thinking that there's no one to take over and he has to sell."

"He knows how much I love the shop. He could have asked me. I mean—" Cleo looked down at her jacket. "Maybe he doesn't like how I run it. He gave me carte blanche to create this individual feel instead of a big chain atmosphere, but maybe I took it in the wrong direction."

"I'm sure that's not it. People love the shop." Emma tapped her arm. "At least gauge his feelings about it, if you want it so much. A little talk to figure out where he's standing can't hurt."

"I guess so." Cleo took a deep breath. "Thanks for the vote of confidence. I'd better get those books wrapped up for the fair. See you later." She dragged the ladder inside.

Emma went to her own door. Her joyful feeling had washed away at Cleo's news, but as the lock clicked open, new energy filled her. This was her very own place. No boss here to tell her what to do. No threat of losing her job and having to start all over again. This was hers, to mold into the business she had dreamed of for years.

She laughed out loud as she pushed the door open and inhaled the scent of chocolate. In the back, snowmen were waiting for their marzipan noses and scarves, while her notebook with ideas for bonbon flavors lay neatly beside the work bench.

And she had an extra reason now to tackle the to-do list head-on. *Just a few more hours and Grant will be picking me up.*

Chapter Six

Grant halted his four-wheel drive outside Emma's shop and looked at his watch. He was early. In the brightly lit shop, customers waited for their turn. But no matter how he angled his head, he couldn't catch a glimpse of Emma behind the counter.

He switched on the radio and tried a few stations, but his mind couldn't focus on news or the Christmas evergreens that cluttered the airwaves. He drummed his fingers on the wheel, then pulled his phone from his pocket and went to his favorite website to look for job postings. There were a few marked with the "newly added" blue banner. *Great.* He clicked on the first one and read the description. A contract for twenty hours a week sounded good, but…international flights. *No.*

The photos of Singapore and Sydney beside the description were enticing, bringing back in an instant the sounds and smells of those faraway places he had loved. But he had seen them all, and his focus had shifted to a whole new perspective. The team he could be with his little girl. Setting up a home base for them somewhere which would be their starting point for amazing adventures.

Movement in the corner of his eye drew his attention back to the little chocolate shop. The door had opened and a young woman with a toddler in a stroller and an older child beside her came out. Framed by the light from within, Emma stood on the doorstep, waving goodbye to them until the trio turned a corner, and then straightened up, inhaling the fresh winter air. Her gaze fell on his car. He leaned to the window and waved at her.

Her smile widened and she waved back. She gestured at the shop and then disappeared. He pocketed the phone and jumped from the car. The lights in the shop went out as she closed up and then she appeared with her coat, scarf and cap in her hand. He already had the passenger door open for her. As she brushed by him, the scent of something sweet wafted toward him. He wasn't sure whether it was chocolate or her perfume. *Maybe chocolate is her perfume?* He had to laugh, and she studied him. "What?"

"You smell just like your shop. Sweet. Ready to go?"

"Sure. Can't wait to see the tree farm."

While he slipped into the driver seat, Emma folded her coat in her lap. The charm bracelet tinkled. He nodded at it. "Cute bracelet."

"Thanks. It's sort of an ongoing project." She touched the tiny whisk with a loving smile. "Every time something momentous happens in my life, I add a charm to it. The book is for graduation, the muffin tray for completing the business course, and the whisk for opening the shop. I don't know yet what the next one will be. Maybe having served my first thousand customers?"

He started the engine. "You must be working like crazy to get everything done and close up shop. I mean, once it's Christmas, you probably want to go spend it with family or friends." He glanced at her, expecting one of her dazzling smiles as she was reminded of her holiday plans.

But Emma's expression tightened. She looked out of the window, fidgeting with her scarf. "I uh...I didn't make any special plans. I don't have parents anymore. They died when I was little. No siblings either. Just me."

"I'm sorry," he said quickly, "that was rude of me." The "*just me*" sounded so sad. As if it wasn't enough. And it wasn't; he knew just how incredibly lonely it could be on your own, even with a little girl sleeping in your arms. But still, she shouldn't think that she was really alone. His head whirled with things to say that would just come out wrong. The only right thing to do would be to reach out for her and put his hand over hers—but he was driving.

"Why would it have been rude?" she asked. "You didn't know."

"That's exactly why. It can bother me how people simply assume things about you and then react from those assumptions, so I should be more tactful."

She looked at him. "You mean because you're a single father?"

"No, because I'm a pilot. They seem to think it's a life full of...excitement." He focused on the street ahead as he navigated the car past a truck and then turned right. "When I tell them my wife died and I'm raising my daughter alone, they are usually at a loss for words."

• • •

Emma didn't know what to say, either. She wanted to know more about how Grant's wife had died, what it had been like for him, but as they knew each other so little, it might be intrusive to ask.

"I guess people just have a lot of prejudices about things.

When I say I was raised in foster care, they sometimes picture me in an orphanage with fifty other kids. But I've always been in families. There were other children, sometimes of the couple who raised me, sometimes other foster children. But it was like a normal home, where I had my own bedroom and got enough attention."

"Still they weren't your parents," he observed quietly.

Emma bit her lip. "No. I will never have my parents." The familiar void twisted inside. More insidious than it had been in the past, it cut into her happiness when she least expected it.

He glanced at her. "I'm sorry I brought it up."

"It's okay. I mean, my father died when I was just a baby so it's not like I ever knew him. And my mother... I do remember things about her, but not a lot. It fades over time. You don't want it to, but it does."

She stared ahead, with a frown. "When I had just been placed in foster care, I worked on my memories of my mother every single day. After school or before bed, I sat in my room and I recalled all of our moments together, trying to etch every little detail about it into my mind. The kitchen floor, the smell of warm cookies, the touch of her hand, the sound of her laughter. I wanted to keep her with me. I was sort of convinced they were all out to make me forget about her, acting like they were my parents now. I'd prove them wrong. But I couldn't keep that up for long. I was too small maybe to have a lot of memories and...I got tired, too. Tired of fighting them, fighting the system that got me transferred again and again."

"How often did you have to move?"

"Eight times, before the family where I was until college." Emma shivered thinking of that little girl with her teddy tucked under her arm, being put on another plane to go to yet another family. "My case is not typical so I'm not saying the system isn't good. Once I was settled in, I had a great childhood. They really loved me. Still do. We call from time to time and I sent them photos of the shop and updates on how I'm doing here. But the start into care was rocky." She turned her face toward him. "Somehow you don't forget." Especially when she was tired or knocked by a setback, the emptiness inside was worse, the sense of drifting alone through the world, never sticking long enough in one place to grow roots, be a part of something. *That's going to change here in Wood Creek. This is a place for staying.*

Grant nodded. His jaw was tight, his eyes pensive. "Being thrown into a whole new situation is a big deal. I can't imagine what it's like for a kid. It's hard enough as a grown-up."

Neither of them spoke as they drove on through the dusk around them, having left the town behind and heading out down a snowy road. Emma wished she'd avoided the truth, made some casual observation about the season being perfect for a little time away or something empty like that. But she also wanted Grant to know. She believed people sometimes changed once they knew about her past. As if their attitude shifted. Feeling sorry for her or thinking she was somehow different. But maybe she hated pity so much she detected it everywhere. And that pesky feeling of not belonging had to shut up for a change.

The charm bracelet moved on her arm, and a smile came up. She might not have parents to buy her charms for it, but she could buy them herself. Remind herself from day to day what she had achieved.

I can do it. Emma sat up as if to imprint the words upon her heart. *I have the shop, my own home over it, and I'm building my dream. The past is over and done with, it's a new beginning.*

• • •

Grant clenched the wheel. He could kick himself for having reminded her of her loss. He wanted her to relax and have fun, like they had this morning in the snow, talking about dogs and making dreams come true. He glanced at her. The thoughtful expression on her face was painful to watch, but he just couldn't stop looking. He wanted to know exactly what she was thinking, feeling.

When Lily had died, he had been in shock, yes, but he had been able to make his own decisions. Leave his job, sell the house, move away. He had been able to take back control any way he knew how.

But Emma had been a child, in the care of others, who had decided for her what was best. Alone with her own thoughts and drawing her own conclusions about the situation.

His heart clenched when he thought of Casey, in tears, a few weeks after Lily's death, asking him, "Didn't she love me anymore?"

"Of course she loved you," he had replied, stunned by her question, racing to figure out how on earth she had gotten that idea into her head.

It had been hard to make out her answer as it had been strangled by her sobbing. But finally, he had pieced it together. "Then why did she leave me if she still loved me?"

Had Emma felt that same way? Abandoned when she had needed her parents most? At least he had been there for Casey to hold her tightly against his heart, even though it hadn't been him she wanted but her mommy who wasn't coming back. Emma hadn't had anyone to hold on to, nothing to rely on as she had been moved from address to address.

Grant inhaled hard and pushed the accelerator.

Emma glanced at him. "It's not safe to go too fast on this icy road."

The purely practical assessment brought him back to reality and immediately he slowed. "Sorry." He clenched the wheel. "I can just get so angry that... Kids shouldn't be going through grief. Not in a major way, you know. I guess we all face setbacks but..."

"Some setbacks are bigger than others," she agreed. She smoothed her scarf across her knees, and her body posture seemed to relax. "I'm sorry if I brought up my parents in a brusque way. I didn't think about how it would be for you. Casey does have you, of course, but she also lost her mother. I guess that was why I wanted to help her when she first came into my shop and asked about the bonbons for you."

"That's okay," he rushed to say. "Please don't apologize. I don't want you to feel like you can't talk to me. That you have to tiptoe around me. Too many people did that. But I can handle it." He added with a rueful grimace, "At least, I can now."

She smiled, but it didn't reach her eyes. "Doesn't it sneak back up on you when you least expect it? I opened up the shop, I was so happy, and I stood in there looking about me and boom, I thought what if my mom could have been here? What if she could hug me now and tell me she was"—her voice quivered—"proud of me?"

Grant swallowed. "I'm sure she would have been."

"I hope so." Emma was silent a moment. "I remember her baking cakes with me. Chocolate cakes, and I could put the frosting on top. I like to think that when she could see me now making my chocolates, she would think I had always had that in me."

Grant nodded. "My wife used to paint with Casey. Lily was an artist. She had her own studio in our home. She worked with charcoal and oil paint and watercolors. There wasn't a lot she couldn't do. She was going to get an exhibition, in an art gallery, just a few weeks from the day she..." He shook his head. "It's crazy but one of the first things I thought when they told me that Lily had passed away was: that can't be, because she has to exhibit her paintings."

Emma didn't say anything. He listened to her quiet breathing beside him, telling him she was still there and waiting for him to continue.

"It was also one of the hardest things to face when I came home. The paintings that were so full of life while she was..." He glanced at her. "I still can't understand that. I guess I don't want to think too much about it. How your life can change in a split second when things go wrong. Up in the air I block all that. If I allow the thought that my plane can fall from the sky, I'd be paralyzed and make bad decisions. Instead, I tell myself that flying is safer than driving. And it works." He laughed softly. "You have no idea what it's like to be up there and feel free. Weightless almost. Not literally of course, there's still gravity, but—things are different. Not as important. I can't wait to get back to it."

"I can imagine. It's wonderful when you do something, and your heart is in it."

Grant nodded. "My parents won't agree, though. They think it's a great arrangement to have me here with Casey. There's always someone to look after her. And I can help out with the tree farm. To them it's the answer to everything."

"But you don't think so?"

"I never meant to stay here." Grant inhaled slowly. He had no idea what she'd think of him if he told her this. *But I need to tell someone.* "I know it sounds selfish. But I needed a place to recuperate. To know for sure that Casey was safe, and I could just...go out among the trees and dig and chop for a day. Until, I was so tired, I couldn't see straight anymore. I just dug and chopped my way through it."

He glanced at her. "I had to create a haven for Casey and find my own feet again. Now I feel like I have. And I need to take that final step. You know, in college I played basketball and I hurt my ankle, couldn't play for a while. When I got back to it, my coach said he could see I moved differently. That I tried to avoid putting my full weight on the ankle. He told me that it's all about trust. That my recovery wasn't complete until the moment when I'd jump and score like I used to, not thinking about the ankle at all. I'm ready for that now. To jump back into life, with Casey. She's my first priority. Always will be."

· · ·

He's ready to move on just as you've met. What kind of timing is that?

Why did her bonds with people always come with an expiration date?

At least you know. And don't you forget it.

They whooshed through a gate with a wooden name tag overhead, reading *Galloway Tree Nursery.* In the distance, friendly light winked at them. Nerves tightened her stomach at the prospect of seeing his parents, his sister Fay and her husband. The entire family around Grant and Casey. He wanted her input on the fair, but would his parents also appreciate a virtual stranger butting in?

She ran a hand through her hair, untangling a few knots. The familiar movement calmed her heartbeat.

You're just here to help. No big deal.

The car halted beside the house, and someone opened the door. Casey ran to the top of the steps leading onto the porch and beamed at her. "You're here! Daddy told me you would be coming."

As soon as Emma got out, Casey grabbed her arm and pulled her down to her level. In a whisper she said, "Do you think the chocolates are working?"

Staring into the girl's excited eyes, Emma struggled for the right answer. "I don't know. But your daddy is very lucky to have such a sweet little girl who wants him to be happy."

Casey nodded. "I thought about making a wish. To put in the Christmas tree at the community center. A wish that Daddy will fall in love with Miss Evelyn."

The bottom fell from Emma's stomach. *A public announcement like that? Half the town reading it and thinking something of it...*

"But I'm not going to do it. That tree doesn't work. Last year I wished for Mommy to come back to us. But she didn't." Casey studied her feet, her expression tight with tension.

Emma's eyes burned. When her mom died, Emma had made the same wish. That everything would return to normal. That she wouldn't be alone anymore. But no matter how many times she had closed her eyes and wished hard that, when she opened them again, she'd be home in their apartment, and Mommy would come in and smile at her, lean down to hug her, it had never happened.

"Hey." Grant appeared and scooped the little girl off her feet into his arms. "I missed you." He held her close and rubbed his cheek over hers. "Got things ready for us?"

Casey nodded. Her eyes lit, and her smile came back full force. "Grandpa is in the big barn." She wriggled to free herself. "Put me down. I want to take Emma there."

Pouting as if he was disappointed that he got so little attention, Grant put Casey down and the girl offered her hand to Emma. The warmth of that trusting grasp seeped deep into her palm. The sad feeling about the past evaporated on the cold air. This place was special to Casey and Grant and they were going to show her around in their kingdom. *Can't wait to see it all...*

Chapter Seven

The big barn turned out to be a tall wooden building with a double door large enough for machines to move in and out. A year was carved into the lintel over the door. 1918. *Just imagine that.* Generations of Galloways had been working this land and building a future for their family here in Wood Creek.

A smaller door sat beside the huge double doors, and Casey pulled Emma through it, into the barn's wide-open space. Electric light from above fell on numerous Christmas trees that had been dug out with their roots still on it or cut off and stood waiting to be transported to customers. The sharp scent of wood and pine mixed with something sweeter. And the cold of the winter air outside also breathed in here, although the tug of the wind was gone, taking the edge off the chill.

Counting quickly how many trees were there, Emma marveled, "What are these still doing here? I thought people bought their tree well in advance."

"Most do," Grant's voice said from behind her. "But

there are always late deciders. Some people even come here on Christmas Eve to pick up a tree, because they suddenly got guests over and are missing a tree, or because they want an extra one to put on their porch or in another room than the living room. All these will be shipped off to the Christmas market in Harker tomorrow afternoon."

"How far are you with preparations for the fair here?" So far, she hadn't seen anything that suggested a Christmas fair with regional attraction was about to take place here on the terrain. *Where are they hiding it?*

"I'll show you in a minute. Let Casey find Grandpa first." He nodded with a grin at the little girl who was running around between the trees looking for her grandfather.

At last, an excited cry rang out and Casey reappeared pulling along a jovial man with a barrel chest and white beard. *The Santa I remembered the moment Casey mentioned the name Galloway to me.*

He smiled at her as he barged over, reaching out his free hand. "Welcome to the tree nursery. I've heard so much about you. Casey told me you have the best shop in the world." He winked. "I asked her if it was even better than the toy shop."

Casey pouted. "Grandpa is mean like that." Then she pressed a kiss on his hand. "But I love him anyway."

Emma blinked against the burn behind her eyes. *If I just had grandparents and could be part of a large family like this.*

Grant said, "Emma wants to see where we'll be setting up the Christmas fair."

Galloway nodded. "Sure. Follow me." He took her through the barn, out of a door on the other side. There was a large open space there, snow covered and kind of desolate.

Emma stared round it, shivering in the chilly breeze and ducking deeper into her coat's upturned collar. She rubbed her hands together and glanced at Galloway. "Here?"

He grinned at her disbelief. "Two days before the fair, a

company will put up the booths. Then we will decorate them and the grounds. You'll see, it's going to be magical."

"Emma can help us with the decorating," Grant said.

She scanned for a response from Galloway, suggesting he didn't agree, but he nodded as if this had been a given from the start.

Casey cheered and took her hand, pulling her into the middle of the area and turning in circles with her, the snow flying up around them. They whirled, faster and faster until they were both dizzy and leaned into each other to stay upright. Casey's giggles echoed against the trees lining the open space like sentries.

A bell dinged, and Casey pricked up her ears. "That's dinner. Grandma is making stew. And maybe we're having chocolate mousse for dessert. Or ice cream. Come on." She grabbed Emma's hand and pulled her along. She stumbled at first, having to adjust to the sudden speed. They ran around the barn, her feet slipping in the snow every few paces. As a kid she had run like that, believing she could almost fly.

The house had brightly lit windows and a hat of snow hanging down from the roof. The door was open, and an elderly woman stood on the threshold waiting for them. Casey let go of Emma and ran up the porch steps, jumping straight into her grandmother's arms. The woman lifted her without effort and hugged her tightly. Then she smiled at Emma. "Hello, welcome to our home. I hope you've got an appetite."

"I do." Emma sniffed the scents coming from the kitchen. Spicy, meaty, invigorating. Her stomach growled. *Seems like lunch was ages ago.*

Grant appeared behind her. He touched her arm a moment as he brushed past her. "Can I take your coat?"

She shrugged out of it and handed it to him, with her scarf. He tucked the scarf into one of the sleeves and hung the coat on the coat rack which was already top heavy with an assortment of coats and work clothes. Underneath several pairs of boots, both rubber and leather, stood waiting to be used. A wooden horse and cart lay discarded beside a yellow bucket to which the sand from summer play still clung. The fullness, with a hint of chaos, contrasted sharply with arrangements in Emma's apartment, where everything had a set place. Neat, convenient.

What would it be like to have a kid around and half-completed puzzles on the floor?

Casey had taken off her own coat and handed it up to her father. Then she followed her grandmother who walked down a few wooden steps leading from the entry into the living room area. The railing beside those steps was entwined in greenery decorated with silver bows and small felt robins.

"I made one in school." Casey pointed at the middle robin. "Gran said we could make more to live here. She also put some on her cards."

"I like making my own Christmas cards. Casey helped me with all the cutting and gluing."

"We also got a lot in the mail. I can open them up and see if we have double ones." Casey gestured up to the long red ribbons threaded from left to right across the room, holding cards with trees, deer, picturesque snowy villages and kids sleighing.

"This is my favorite." Casey ran to stand underneath an extra-large card of puppies tucked into stockings. "I'm also asking Santa for a puppy."

"Show Emma into the kitchen." Grant ruffled his daughter's hair. She ducked out from under his hand and ran through an archway that gave access to a large kitchen. The long oak table on the far end offered room for at least ten people. The surface was full of little dents and scratches. *Had Grant sat there doing homework? Did he ride that rocking horse in the corner, pluck the hairs from its half-gone tail?*

Everything in this kitchen seemed to tell a story, was part of a family legacy. Emma had never had something like that. No pieces of furniture passed on from a gran, no photos in an album to which she could add her own. Just her bracelet on her arm, recording her life, without any connection to other people's lives.

But it is my *life,* my *story to write.* Maybe that newspaper photo hadn't been picture perfect, but it represented her new beginning.

"Come sit with me," Casey called to her, slipping into the wooden bench built against the wall and patting the pillows with an embroidered snowflake pattern. "These are the winter ones. In spring we have magnolia and in summer poppies. Gran makes them on a machine."

Mrs. Galloway winked at Emma. "There goes the illusion that it's all handmade."

"Your secret is safe with me." She ran a finger across the pattern. "The stitching is so delicate."

"Let me know if I can make you something. It's my escape when I can't face another tree. That, and cooking." Mrs. Galloway extracted a large orange pan from the oven.

"When I cook for myself, I usually choose something quick and easy. Noodles, a salad. But this smells like the flavors really had time to soak in."

"You're welcome to drop by for dinner after a busy day." Mrs. Galloway gestured around the table. "It's open house here."

"Maybe Emma would like to cook together with you sometime." Grant slid into the space beside her. He leaned over to her and added in a whisper, "Since you loved to do that with your mom. Of course, nothing can replace her, but you might like to give it a go again. If you want to." He broke off awkwardly and picked up a piece of bread from the breadbasket. His mother shook her head at him, putting the orange pan in place. "Wait until everybody is here and Grandpa has said grace, Grant."

Emma suppressed a grin when Grant obediently put the bread on his plate. She whispered to him, "Thanks for the offer. I'll think about it."

There was a bustle in the living room area, and two more people entered the kitchen, a woman in her thirties with dark hair and brown eyes and a blond man of about the same age, with a quiet smile as he looked around at the people present. "This is our daughter Fay and her husband Bob," Mr. Galloway said as he dried his hands with a thick red towel. "Fay, Bob, this is Emma from the chocolate shop in town."

"Oh, I've heard so much about the shop," Fay enthused as she leaned over the table to shake Emma's hand. "I really have to pop round sometime. But December is crazy busy for us, with the fair coming up and all."

Bob tried to lift the lid off the pan on the table, but his mother-in-law slapped him on the fingers with the oven glove she had just taken off. "No peeking. Now, everybody, take your places."

They all sat down, Galloway at the head of the table, his wife on his right hand, Fay and Bob beside her, opposite Casey, Emma and Grant.

"Let's join hands," Mr. Galloway said in his deep, warm voice.

Emma's stomach tightened as Grant opened his hand palm up for her to put her hand into. *This is a private family moment.*

But when she reluctantly placed her hand in his, his fingers closed around hers with a surprisingly careful touch.

Galloway prayed, "Thank you, Father, for your love shown to us today, giving us the strength to do our work and put food on this table. We thank you for keeping us all together and bringing Emma in our midst. Bless us all by your grace. Amen."

"Amen," everybody echoed and then there was a clatter of china as they picked up their plates to hold out for Mrs. Galloway to fill. She lifted the lid off the pan, and the spicy aroma Emma had detected earlier intensified. Inside the pan, generous chunks of meat and vegetables of various colors swam in a thick sauce. Mrs. Galloway gave her two spoonfuls and then mashed potatoes to go with it.

Grant passed her the breadbasket.

They ate in silence, especially the men tucking into the meal with relish, while Casey was the only one who kept chattering, about some craft project she had done at school. The name Miss Evelyn recurred every few sentences and Emma peeked at Grant to see if he showed any interest in the teacher. He seemed to notice her surreptitious glances and winked at her.

Emma quickly lowered her eyes to the stew on her plate. It warmed her inside out, even heating her cheeks.

• • •

It was rather unreal to see Emma sitting at his family's kitchen table—and still it was somehow right. They often had guests for dinner and some people simply didn't seem to fit very well into their rather simple rustic lifestyle. Those people felt uncomfortable, talking too loud about their agenda or their holiday plans at some all-inclusive tropical island resort. But Emma sat there as if she had always been there, responding to a remark by Fay with a story about her shop, the deliveries.

Grant chimed in about the snow dogs they had made, and Casey asked if she could see them. Grant said, "Maybe we can make new ones for the fair."

He glanced at Emma. She gave a quick nod and smile

before looking at Bob, who asked a question about how she had ended up on Heart Street. It was convenient that the others asked some of the things Grant also wanted to know and he could just quietly eat and watch her as she told her story, watch the little movements in her face, the way she rested her hands on the table's edge or gestured with them. "Cleo has some great ideas for Valentine's Day and maybe my chocolate can also play a part in that. It'll be February before you know it."

"Oh, is Mr. Fellows keeping the shop open?" Fay asked. "I heard he's retiring."

"I heard that too, but Cleo has so many plans," Emma said. "There must be some way to keep the shop open."

"Outside investors?" Grant suggested.

"In Wood Creek?" Bob scoffed.

Grant gave him a "come on" look. No need to make Emma feel like a shop on Heart Street was a dead horse. It was bad enough her next-door neighbor who had helped her settle in would be leaving.

With Cleo gone, who will look after Emma? Ensure she takes breaks and does sign up for that book club she claims to be too busy for?

"Let her eat," Grant's father chimed in. "I'm ready for second servings already, and she's not even halfway through."

Emma flushed. "I'm not a big eater."

"That's fine," Grant's mother said. "Eat what you want. Now give me your plate, hungry wolf." She picked up her husband's plate to refill it.

Casey laughed. "Are you a wolf, Grandpa? What am I then? A wolf cub?"

"I don't think so." Fay shook her head. "I think you would sooner be a little deer, running through the forest."

"What about you?" Casey asked Emma. "What animal are you?"

Emma considered the question with a deep frown.

"Daddy would be a bird," Casey said. "He loves to fly and see things from above. He always says they are much prettier when you see them from up high."

His mother stirred uncomfortably. He wasn't sure if she suspected he was looking into jobs, making plans to leave again, or if she just didn't like to be reminded of the risks of his career. She had never been a fan of his flying, thinking he would one day crash. And now that he was a single father…

Is she right? Do I have to change careers, choose something different, safer? A job on the ground? Everything inside of him fought against the idea. *I need to fly. My place is up there.*

"You'd be an eagle," Casey said with a satisfied nod. She focused on Emma again. "Do you already know what you'd be? There is no animal that makes chocolates. Is there?"

Bob hid a grin behind his hand. No one here would ever laugh at Casey, making her feel like something she said was silly. They all wanted her to have imagination, to think about the world, to feel her way into it, without being afraid she was considered an oddball.

"I think you'd be a butterfly," Casey said suddenly. "They do fly but not as high. They stay close to the flowers they sit on. And they are very pretty."

And very fragile. You don't touch butterflies, or you damage them.

His stomach tightened, and he got to his feet in a rush and started to gather the empty plates, ignoring his mother's surprised look. Bob asked Casey if she had a little room left for dessert and Fay got up to fetch something from the pantry. She came back with a big bowl his mother used to make ice cream. Grant leaned over to Fay to see inside. "Oh, banana! Who wants some homemade banana ice cream?"

The "me, me" rang around the table, and his mother

brought out the chocolate sprinkles to put on top.

Casey put some on her hand and used them to create a pattern on her ice cream. "Can you see what it is, Daddy?" She held out her bowl to him past Emma.

A heart. He cleared his throat. "Is it a Christmas tree?"

"No! Look better."

"A dog?"

"No, it doesn't have legs."

"A balloon."

"Noooo." Casey retracted the bowl and dug her spoon into the ice cream. "It's all melting."

Saved by the bell.

Fay started a conversation about the fair and soon they were finalizing some details for the booths, while his mother made after dinner coffee.

With their coffee they all moved to the leather couches in the living room area, grouped around the hearth. His mother lit the candles on the low table, waving off Emma's offer to help with the dishes. "I have a dishwasher I'll turn on later." They sat down together, and Casey decided the game of the night was charades. "We play in teams. We'll be Team Eagle. Daddy, me and you."

Fay explained, "One of us acts out the fairytale and the other team members have to guess. If you can't guess it in time, the other teams get a chance."

"I'll keep the score," Grant's father said, holding up a notebook and pencil.

Fay set an alarm on her phone. "Two minutes per fairytale. Teams have to split up across the room so they can discuss without the others overhearing."

Grant waved Emma along to the sofa while Casey took the center of the room to start her enactment. She walked around with a benign smile, waving at people around her. "Princess," Grant whispered to Emma. His shoulder touched hers a moment. "Or queen."

"The evil queen?" Emma whispered back. Out loud, she said to Casey, "Is it Snow White?"

Casey shook her head and stopped walking through the room. She looked about her and yawned. Then she lay down on the floor and closed her eyes.

"Sleeping Beauty," Grant called.

Casey shook her head more emphatically. She turned onto one side, then the other.

"I have no idea." Grant glanced at Emma. "You?"

"Maybe." Emma slipped to the edge of the sofa, following Casey's every movement. The girl sat up again, feeling underneath her with a pained expression.

"The Princess and the Pea," Emma called.

"Yessss." Casey jumped to her feet. "You're so smart. Daddy would never have guessed."

"Thanks a lot," Grant muttered. Emma poked him with her elbow. "Time to brush up on your knowledge of Hans Christian Andersen."

"That guy just wrote too much."

"Team change." Casey ran over and leaned against him, while Bob galloped through the room, tossing his head and making neighing noises. He halted and looked up at something.

"Sleeping Beauty," Fay called. "You're the prince coming to her castle to kiss her awake."

"No." Bob put his head in his neck as if he was looking up at something that reached all the way into the skies.

"You can't talk," Casey scolded him. "Just shake your head." She looked at Emma and whispered, "Do you know what it is?"

"Jack and the Beanstalk?" Fay chewed her lip, watching her husband stare at the ceiling overhead.

Bob shook his head and gestured with his hands as if

something was falling over him.

"I know." Fay sat up. "Uh, the woman who can make it snow. What's her name?" She pressed a hand against her temple as if to help her remember.

"Time is running out," Galloway warned.

"Come on." Bob gestured furiously as if he was pulling something over him and then grabbing at it. He pointed up.

"Does he mean you're getting closer?" Grant wondered aloud.

"No, I've got it." The excitement in Emma's voice made him sit up. She pulled Casey to her and whispered something in her ear.

The alarm sounded. "Time's up." Bob scowled at Fay. "It wasn't that hard, really. Other takers?"

Casey raised her hand. She waited a moment for full effect before saying with a dramatic gesture, "Rapunzel. She threw her hair off the tower so the prince could climb up."

Grant pursed his lips to keep his features in check. He didn't dare look at Emma. If he saw her struggle as well, he'd burst out laughing.

He high-fived Casey. "Team Eagle strikes again."

"That late?" Bob checked his watch. "I gotta call Ed about the tractor. I don't think you want to use the workroom tonight?" Without waiting for Grant's answer, he rushed up the stairs, two steps at a time.

"What about my team?" Fay protested. "Now I'm left all alone." She looked at Casey. "Are you coming to me?"

Casey shook her head. "We won." She ran off to the cupboard and fetched three plastic crowns with elastic bands attached. "We have to wear these all night." She gave Emma one and crawled into Grant's lap to put the crown on his head personally.

Emma slipped the plastic band under her chin and tilted her head. "How do I look?"

"Hmmm." Grant surveyed the crooked angle of the dented crown. Her eyes shone at him with a hint of laughter left over Rapunzel. "Just perfect."

He stretched his legs, hugging his daughter who rested her face in the crook of his neck. *Everything about this night is perfect.*

Funny how a virtual stranger fit into his family like she had always been there.

Chapter Eight

No marzipan for me tonight. Booths and glitter. I can't wait.

Emma locked up the shop and walked the few paces to her front door. Stepping into her hallway, she almost slipped on the mail lying on the doormat. She picked up two bills and a green envelope decorated with star stickers. The upper left corner said Sonya Daniels, one of her foster sisters. *Haven't talked to her in ages.*

She tore the envelope open with her little finger and pulled out a 3D Christmas card. Inside, neat handwriting said, *This is the season of love for us as we went from two to three.* A photo pasted underneath showed a beaming Sonya holding a tiny baby and her dark-haired husband Norman locking them both in a solid embrace. The text went on: *Born on December 10, David Matthew Daniels. Our Christmas miracle.*

She couldn't take her eyes off that tiny face, the small hands held against the cheeks, the look of utter bliss in the parents' eyes. *Sonya, who I played pirates with, is now a mom.* It was amazing how an uncertain little girl who had liked to hide under the bed had changed into this confident grown-up with her own family. *All because of love.*

Could it also change her life around, if she let it?

She blinked and forced her mind to something practical. She'd have to send Sonya and Norman a cute card to congratulate them. Maybe she could make some kind of baby-related chocolate and send it along? *Might also be an idea to add to the offer. Baby carriages decorated with pink or blue frosting.*

The clock in the living room chimed and she startled, dropping the card and the bills on the table. She still had to change, and Grant could be here any minute. In her tiny bedroom she threw her work outfit aside. On the bed was her new pink woolen hat with silver threading waiting for its first outing. Her trusty pink fleece, practical gray jeans and sturdy black ankle boots were perfect for the job. In the ankle boots she could wear double socks so her feet wouldn't get cold standing in the snow. She still wasn't sure how they were going to change that barren piece of snowy land into a magical fairground. *Guess I'm about to find out.*

Leaving the house in a rush, she almost bumped into Mrs. Beaver. "I just wanted to ring," the woman said, pointing at her doorbell.

The fluttery feeling in Emma's stomach at her outing tonight died an instant death as she faced the woman who hadn't even wanted to look at her chocolates when she had delivered them to her home. *What's wrong?*

"Uh, yes, well…I uhm…" Mrs. Beaver said. She didn't seem to know exactly how to begin.

Tell her you don't have time for her now. She can come back later.

No. She straightened up. *I want to know what it's about. And I won't agree to a refund. I made what she asked for.* Despite her determination, her legs were wobbly, and she fidgeted with her key.

"I wanted to say I'm sorry," Mrs. Beaver said at last. "I barely looked at your creations when you delivered them, because I was in an awful rush to get everything done. I had made a mistake with the batter, so I had to redo it and my head was just full of worries about the night. Later on, I did look and...they were so very artfully crafted. My friends all said they had never seen anything like it."

"Really? Oh, thank you."

"I could have paid a little more attention when you brought them. Made a compliment about the effort you put into them. I didn't realize..." She looked Emma in the eye and said, "I just want you to know that—we very much enjoyed them, and I want to do business with you more often." She handed her an envelope. "The extra is for your effort."

"Thank you, I'm happy to hear that."

Mrs. Beaver nodded firmly. "We should all support the small businesses here on the street. It's hard enough to keep afloat these days. So many shops having to close." She nodded at the bookshop. "I heard Mr. Fellows is thinking of retiring soon and we'll lose our bookshop. We can go to another town of course, but it isn't the same. And people shouldn't start with me about how nice it is to be ordering online. All those websites are what ruined it for the real shops in the first place."

She shook her head. "Sad when you think about how in the past when people had so little money, they were loyal to the local shopkeepers and everyone could make a living and these days when people have so much more to spend, they all want the cheapest offer and let the small businesses go bankrupt."

Emma wanted to say something, but Mrs. Beaver didn't give her a chance. "I feel strongly about supporting local businesses and I also tell that to all my friends. Good day."

And she marched off.

Emma stared after her and then laughed. Mrs. Beaver's approach was a bit brusque maybe, but it came from a good heart. *Hopefully, her friends will wait a few days to place their orders so I can keep up.*

A car horn honked. She looked for Grant's car but didn't see it. Someone waved from the open window of a station wagon. It was Fay. "Grant is busy helping Dad and Bob with the booths. The company arrived awfully late and they expect the customer to chip in getting it all done."

Emma nodded as she slipped into the passenger seat beside her and buckled up. "Thanks for giving me a lift."

"No problem. I'm glad you want to help. Decorating all those booths is some job. It's fun, but I can tell you that after having done a dozen you want to scream at the sight of yet another Christmas ornament."

Emma laughed. "I make chocolates every day and still I've got more ideas than I can work on. I write a lot down in my notebook, with little sketches of how it's going to look."

"Mom's the same with her embroidery. Only her sketches are not neatly in a notebook but scribbled on the back of receipts and grocery lists which then get misplaced. You should see her digging through drawers to recover some all-important design. Hey, look out." Fay hit the brakes for a couple of kids running into the street chasing each other with handfuls of snow. Shaking her head, she accelerated again, only to stop a few yards down for a young mother with a double buggy, straining under the weight of too many shopping bags. Colorful presents half stuck out of the bags, the glittery bows on them ruffling on the breeze.

"Do you like Christmas shopping?" Fay asked Emma.

Emma shrugged. "I don't have that many people I buy gifts for. I do send cards. Usually I make them myself, but this year I bought them ready made. I just don't have the time for card making with the shop and all." Still this was the second night in a single week she wasn't diving into fondant and ganache but going out. As if it wasn't just her and the shop anymore.

She shifted uncomfortably in the seat. *Decorating for the fair counts as work, right?*

"Is your family coming over for Christmas?" Fay asked. "Or maybe you're flying out?"

"I have no family to speak of, so I'll just stay here and enjoy my time off."

"You could spend Christmas Eve with us. I didn't want to interfere with any plans you might already have made, that's why I asked." Fay looked uncomfortable, biting her lip.

"I'd love to," Emma rushed to say. "If it's okay with your family. I don't want to intrude."

Is this smart? a voice in the back of her head whispered. *Making more memories with Grant and Casey when they are leaving…*

Time was running out like it had during the game of charades. She wanted to embrace every moment, also knowing it would make it extra hard later on. *But it isn't just about Grant and Casey. Fay is asking me to come over. And I really want to cook with Mrs. Galloway sometime or bake a cake.*

But…would it be the same after Grant had gone? Could she sit at that kitchen table, having dinner, feeling the emptiness of the place beside her where Grant had been? Miss the warmth of his fingers around hers as they bowed their heads for prayer?

Even worse: hear stories about how he's doing, how happy he is, far away from Wood Creek?

Casey wanted him to be happy, right? He'll have his flying, and you'll have his family as friends right here near the shop. Perfect outcome for everybody.

She forced her hands to relax, palms up, and took a deep breath. *Get busy and get out of your head.*

. . .

Grant leaned against the booth as he reached up with both hands to attach the greenery with thin metal wire to the upper post. His shoulders ached from making this same movement over and over. He didn't want to count how many booths he had left to do. This was just part of the setup process. Then the fun stuff would begin.

An engine hummed in the distance. *Already?* Fay had done it quickly. He had hoped to be done by the time Emma arrived on the scene.

"Hey!" he yelled to Bob who was busy a few booths down. "If you finish up attaching the greenery, I'll get started on the other stuff."

Bob waved in acknowledgment, and Grant hurried to the entry to the fair area to meet Fay and Emma. The snow patterns on her fleece and the threading on her hat sparkled, but the real eye-catcher was her smile.

She waved and he signaled back, forcing his legs to go faster. Stopping in front of her, he had to catch his breath before he could speak. Apparently, the work had taken more of a toll than he had noticed. "We're almost done with the greenery so you can help with the details. There are boxes over there…" He sucked in cold air.

Emma put a hand on his arm. "Take it easy. You're pushing yourself too hard."

The worry in her eyes struck a chord inside that hadn't been touched in ages. He worried for Casey, but nobody worried for him, asked him how he was doing, how he was feeling, if he was maybe pushing himself too hard. Well, yeah, his mother did say he should take care, but she was his mother. Since he had become single, nobody ever reached out to the deepest part of him like...a partner, an equal in a relationship you built.

"The boxes over there," he gestured to a line of them on wooden planking, "contain ornaments and bows. Every booth's greenery has to be decorated with a few."

"And every booth gets two lanterns," Fay added, who had come up and stood with them now. "They are great for atmosphere and have glass all around, so the sparks can't get out and set anything on fire. I'm going to help Bob a sec."

She rushed away, sliding across a bit of frozen snow, her arms stretched to balance herself. The large electric lights which had been put to provide light for them to work in illuminated the area like a stage.

Grant and Emma stood there, looking at each other. The silent forest loomed close, with its snow-powdered branches and icicles. The skies stretched overhead, deep blue with a hint of orange, encasing everything in a great universe of beauty. He wanted to point out the stars to her, but to talk would be to somehow break it. *Just be with me.*

"Let's get started," she suggested.

"Sure." He guided her to the first box and pointed out what she might select. "One booth can't have three stars and another none, so it has to be split kind of evenly."

"Okay." Emma looked quickly across the contents of the various boxes and selected a few ornaments and bows. Where the various patterns and details were all a bit much to him, and he selected for shapes only, she made choices that were somehow a perfect match and created a whole.

Across the crunching snow they went to the first booth. She was just able to reach up and attach the decorations, but Grant said, "I'll get you a step," and ran to fetch it. Sucking the cold air deep into his lungs, he had to suppress the urge to jump as he went. It felt good to be alive.

When he came back with the step, Emma was already at the second booth. Her expression was full of deeply serious concentration, but her eyes sparkled, betraying she also enjoyed it. Silvery glitter sat on her cheek. He put the step ready for her. "Anything else you need?"

"Not right now. I've got the color scheme all worked out: silver and red for this booth, then golden for the next, then blue and white. These little see-through ornaments are the greatest."

She leaned forward to scoop the hook attached to the ornament around a twig. "Come on." She perched on her toes, angling sideways, and pitched over. With a yelp she almost crashed onto the booth's wooden counter.

Grant grabbed her round the waist and steadied her. "Careful now." His heart thundered so hard it droned in his ears. "Did you hurt yourself?"

"No. All good now." She smiled down at him. "Thanks."

He held her just a moment longer, inhaling the perfume wafting from her fleece jacket. Sweetness, chocolate. Something uniquely Emma.

"I'm glad you came," he said.

• • •

Emma stared into Grant's deep brown eyes. He was holding her, and he was saying he enjoyed her company.

At least that's what he means by saying he's glad I came, right? Her brain didn't seem to function as it usually did. She could focus on one thing only: the warmth in his eyes. Something even deeper than that, which forced her to keep looking, unable to glance away.

Her head went light with excitement. If he hadn't steadied her, she might have tipped backward. The night closed in around them, but the lights put up still created a circle of light in which she stood like the princess in a fairytale and wished this moment could last forever.

He's going to lift me off the step, put me down in the snow in front of him and lean over—

She widened her eyes. *No. Don't think that or want that. He's leaving soon. It'll just ruin everything if you let him make you feel so alive whenever he's near. This is not a fairytale. Don't be silly, don't daydream.*

"Could you get me more bows?" she said hoarsely. "Red velvet or satin."

He nodded and let go of her and walked away. The wind breathed around her and drove goose bumps out on her arms. A shiver came up from her toes, and even her face felt suddenly numb. Every fiber of her wanted him to come back and hold her again, but her heart beat in a staccato warning rhythm.

This isn't real. It can't work out. He's like the Christmas glitter: only here for a short time. January will wipe it away.

• • •

Why has she gone so quiet?

Grant surveyed Emma from the side. Her facial expression was pensive while she attached the ornaments and velvet bows, her posture a bit tight. *Maybe because she almost fell earlier? If she hurt herself, bruised her wrist, it would be a problem with her business.*

"Done," Emma said, stepping back to judge the booth. "I really like the combination of red and gold."

"You did a great job," he agreed. "You should have been an interior designer."

"I always liked creating things, like making clothes for paper dolls or cutting pictures from lifestyle magazines and creating a dream house." She smiled, and at the same time sadness flashed in her eyes.

"*Your* dream house?"

Emma sighed. "I just wanted to have a place of my own. In foster care you usually share the parents with other kids. With their own kids even. You can't help but feel that…they must love their own children more. It's unreasonable, I know, and I don't blame them, because they tried really hard to treat us all equally. But that is not the way I felt. I was always dreaming about a house somewhere where I could live with my real parents. Or with a family of my own."

She looked down with a frown as if she tried to search deep inside of herself. "This whole dating thing, especially online, seems to be so superficial. Just about who is better looking or has more money. A house, a boat. I feel like I can't compete."

"You don't have to," he said. "You're okay the way you are."

Emma smiled up at him. "Thanks, but it doesn't feel that way. You always have to prove yourself. Be interesting, daring. Go places." She laughed softly. "I've never traveled. I haven't been to Paris. I can't post pictures of Venice. I bet you've been to all those cities, lots of times."

"Sure, but that was for work. And sometimes there was so little time to have a look around. Take Tokyo." He enumerated on his fingers. "Long flight to get there. Return is the next day. Touch of jetlag because of the time difference. It all adds up sooner to resting at the hotel than sightseeing. And after a while, you even get a bit jaded. Like I've already seen this, I've done this before."

Emma nodded. "That's what I mean. I met a lot of men at the business seminar I went to."

The idea was unsettling, but he refused to analyze why.

"They were nice enough when we sat down to lunch, but they were all talking about their trips and their hobbies. I felt like I just couldn't keep up. I don't play tennis or golf. I don't go on wine tasting courses. I even wondered if I was cut out to be a business owner. If it involved all of those things—"

"That makes no sense," he retorted with energy. "A business owner is someone who owns a business and knows how to take care of it. To make great chocolate you don't need to know how to golf. Don't change. Stay the way you are."

Emma's eyes lit up a moment, then she looked away. "I think we're done, but should we try the lanterns? At least at one booth to see if they are in the right position to give a bit of atmospheric light?"

"You're right." He dug into his pocket for a lighter he had snatched from the kitchen earlier.

Emma carefully opened the little door of the lantern to the left and Grant inserted his hand and flicked the lighter on. The fire grabbed the wick of the candle and a flame broke to life, quivering on the breeze.

She leaned over to look at the flame inside. It reflected in her eyes, and off the glitter on her cheeks and chin. Her features softened, and he couldn't take his eyes off her. She smiled as if to encourage that little flame and even touched the glass with her finger. If he had done this alone, he would have rushed over it, taking a quick look, right, everything okay, then would have blown it out again. But Emma grabbed the opportunity to see a spark of Christmas already.

She looked up at him. "The other one as well?"

"Sure." Anything to linger, live the moment.

They shifted to the other side of the booth and lit the lantern there. Its circle of light touched the circle coming from the left lantern and the warm glow seemed perfect in the snowy world. Grant inhaled the scent of pine from the trees further away, that touch of burning wick and wax of the candles. Fresh snow was drifting from above, gently descending on Emma's hat and shoulders, one flake after another, tender ice crystals decorating her. He leaned over and brushed a bit of snow off her shoulder, showed her his hand. "They are all different if you look closely. You should really see them under a microscope or a camera with a micro lens."

Emma looked up at him with a smile. "You always want to bring in something to analyze it."

Grant held her gaze. "Really?"

"Yes. I think it's your pilot background. You want to know all the rules and the route and the patterns and the risks to keep all those people you're flying around safe."

He had to laugh. "You're probably right. I love to plan. Not just my flying, but my climbing as well. The best equipment, the safest route to the top. Excellent guides, the fullest preparation."

"Climbing?" She sounded a touch surprised and half worried.

"I used to go out with friends a lot. Before my wife died. After that, I had Casey to look after, didn't want to leave her alone for a stretch of time. But I do intend to get back to it. It's the best feeling in the whole world to stand on a mountain peak knowing you conquered it."

• • •

Emma tried to keep chatting normally. But disbelief churned inside of her, muddling her thoughts. *One moment it's like we understand each other and then, bam, you wipe it all away with your climbing.* Why couldn't it have been some low-key, no risk hobby like bowling or playing darts?

If she had come across him online, she would have clicked on his picture for sure. Drawn in by his strong features and to-melt-for eyes, but as soon as she would have read about his job and hobbies, she would have returned to the list to search for someone safer.

Grant Galloway would have been nothing for her. She was someone who liked to stay at home, putter in the garden if there was one, cook, bake, sit in the sun with a book. She didn't need to go out and conquer the world. They really were polar opposites.

So what? Friends can be different and still support each other. Even after he leaves.

She shivered.

"You're getting cold," Grant said. "We better go inside. Do you want to blow out the candles?"

Emma nodded and opened the door. She lowered her face to the opening and blew. The flame resisted at first, flickering to life again, but as she persisted, it quenched. *See. You can also conquer your attraction to Grant. Try a little harder.*

But I don't want to.

As the second lantern died, the cold electric light from above bathed the booths, turning the snow even whiter and chillier, seeping into the very core of her with its icy touch. *I don't want to lose him.*

She shivered again, and Grant put his arm around her shoulders. "Better walk fast to warm up already. I think Fay will have hot chocolate for us."

Fay and Bob had left them completely to themselves. *On purpose?* Emma's cheeks heated. Did they hope Grant would grow to like her and stick around town? Having seen their family dynamics, she could guess they would love to keep him close. She wanted that too, to lean into him as they walked back to the house. But she had to keep walking on her own two feet.

If he wanted to leave town, he would. *And that's good. No point keeping him here against his will. He should be happy. That was Casey's wish.*

Chapter Nine

"More marshmallows?" Fay asked, holding the bag out in her direction.

Emma shook her head. "If I have any more, I'm going to turn into one."

"White or pink? I would be pink." Casey laughed. She lay on her stomach on the sheepskin in front of the fireplace in which a log fire crackled around freshly cut wood. Grant had brought it in after dinner and taken his time to build the perfect fire. He had even explained to her how to do it, but it had been a bit lost on her as the memory had replayed in her head of the moment she had almost fallen, and he had caught her. The safest place in the world had to be in his arms.

Grant checked his watch. "About bedtime, Casey."

"Aaaaah, Daddy!" Casey rolled onto her back, pulling a plaid from the rocking chair across herself as if to hide under, become invisible.

With a smooth movement Grant came to his feet and went over. "I'm looking for Casey. Where can she be? She's all gone. Has she hidden behind the couch?" He crouched behind it, feeling with his hands across the floor. "No, she is not here."

Bursts of giggles came from underneath the plaid giving Casey away, but Grant continued his systematic search of the living room, even opening the buffet's door to see if Casey was hiding inside.

While he was busy with that, Casey crawled away from the fire, under her plaid cover, taking up a new spot behind her grandfather's chair.

Grant straightened up and rolled back his shoulders. "Where is she? Has anybody seen her?"

He let his gaze drift by his parents, sister and brother-in-law who all maintained puzzled or innocent expressions. Then his eyes met Emma's. Electricity shocked through her upon the contact, the moment she looked full into that chocolate warmth. His smile deepened just a bit. For a moment, she wondered what it would be like if this was their house and he was chasing Casey and they would take her to bed together and then return here and sit on the sheepskin, her leaning into him and him locking his arms around her and kissing the top of her head. Togetherness, belonging.

She widened her eyes for a second to bring herself back to reality.

Grant's eyes seemed to question her. "I haven't seen Casey," she said a little too loud.

He prowled through the room, looking behind the bookcases in the far corner. Casey was moving again, trying to scuttle behind the couch where he had already looked. But then Grant turned around suddenly and cried, "I see you! I'm coming for you!"

Casey shrieked and fled. Grant ran through the room and grabbed Casey, plaid and all, lifted her high and held her in his arms. Her laughter filled the room.

Emma's eyes pricked at the idea of feeling so safe with

someone, so sheltered, so loved.

Grant lowered Casey to the floor. "Up to bed, little one." He gave her a gentle shove toward the stairs and after a long sigh, she dropped the plaid and made her way up, stopping to wave at all of them and give them kiss hands. "I love you, Gramps. I love you, Gran. I love you, Fay and Bob." Her footfalls raced up the stairs.

Grant followed to tuck her into bed, and Mrs. Galloway asked if anyone wanted a cup of tea. Counting the raised hands, she disappeared into the kitchen area to make some. Emma ambled after her to sneak a peek at her teapot collection.

Christmas Eve would be the perfect occasion for a gift. She scanned the shelf on which the teapots sat. An English double decker bus, a cottage in the snow, and an owl. *Nothing with chocolate. If I can find one online that has some sort of link to my shop, it would make a perfect personal present.*

Grinning at her little secret, she returned to sit by the fire.

"You can give me a tip." Fay came over and showed Emma a magazine. "I spotted the perfect spring coat but what color do I choose? Light blue or soft yellow? I'm worried about it getting stained quickly."

"Let me see." Emma leaned over the magazine. Her ears scanned the sounds in the room for footfalls coming back from above. Grant joining them again.

Newspaper pages rustled while Mr. Galloway turned them and commented on a headline.

In the kitchen, the kettle began to sing as the water reached boiling point. A clank of china on the sink and a pantry door closing, probably when Mrs. Galloway collected the cookie jar. *Not what I want to hear.*

But wait. There. He's coming. As the footfalls beat down the stairs, Emma kept looking at the colorful pictures Fay was pointing out to her, but her thoughts couldn't quite focus on spring colors and the possibility of stains.

"Emma."

She startled upright at his voice.

"Casey wants to say good night to you." He pointed up the stairs with a wide inviting gesture. "To the right. The door with all the flowers pasted on it."

Emma rose to her feet, then hesitated. "Are you sure it's okay?"

"Sure. Go on up. She said she wanted to see you *alone* so..." He winked at her. "Maybe she's got a secret to share?"

Emma's cheeks flushed. That first encounter with Grant, face to face, in her shop, where he had quizzed her about his daughter's chocolate order, had been rather awkward. *No new plans, please.*

She went up the stairs, holding on to the railing, well aware of the growing height behind her. Open stairs gave her a dizzying sensation of tipping backward and falling down. But Grant climbed mountains and dangled down cliff sides, relying on a few ropes to hold his weight.

Upstairs, she went to the door with the paper sunflowers pasted on it and knocked. Casey's voice called, a little muffled, "Come in!"

She entered and wanted to leave the door open, but Casey gestured to her from the bed. "Close the door. Daddy can't hear it."

Another secret. Oh, no.

With a hammering heart, Emma closed the door.

Casey waved her over and patted the bed's edge. "Sit down. I'm so glad you're here. You can help me. You see..." She frowned hard. Her fingers played with the pink duvet. "Daddy always says you have to try new things even though you think they're scary because new things always are and if you never tried, you'd never learn anything or get anywhere. At the fair there is a stage and bands play and people can sing Christmas songs. And I want to sing a song. I think it's scary with all the people looking at me, but I want to try. For Daddy."

Emma's heart melted at the pride in the little girl's eyes.

"You have to help me practice. I already know what song I'm going to do. 'Silent Night.' I know all the words. I just have to get it right."

"Get what right?"

"How it sounds." Casey eyed her worriedly. "It's not right. Not how it's supposed to."

She took a deep breath and started to sing, too high pitched and brittle. Her nerves were obvious, making her voice quiver. She had to draw breath halfway each line and rushed the next words to make it fit.

Casey stopped after one couplet and said, "It's not very good, is it?" Her eyes seemed enormous in her pale face.

Emma's arms itched to reach out and wrap that little girl in a hug. *Tell her she doesn't have to do it. That you wouldn't dare, either.*

Relief rushed through her at the idea that something potentially disastrous could be avoided.

But how would Casey feel on the day of the fair, looking at the stage where she could have stood? Happy or rather disappointed she hadn't even tried? After all, Daddy had told her to try new things.

"How about giving it another go? You have to warm up your voice first. You have to do exercises for it." She tried to remember what the choir director in college had told them. She hadn't sung in ages. "You have to do like aaaaaaaah…" She held the tone while opening her mouth wide and closing it further, forming an o with her lips or shaking her head so it sounded all weird.

Casey fell backward on the bed laughing.

That's better. "Honestly," Emma said, feigning to be

hurt. "All big singers do it."

Casey sat up again. "I want to try." She opened her mouth wide and went *aaaaaah*, pulling the weirdest faces as she was at it. Emma had to laugh no matter how much she tried to suppress it. Casey grinned at her. "See, it's weird."

"But it helps. And it will also help if you have the right attitude while you sing. Stand up, relax your shoulders and breathe from your stomach." Emma rose to her feet and showed her. "The better you stand, the better it will sound. Now come over here and try again."

"Okay." Casey came to stand beside her in her pink pajamas on her bare feet and started "Silent Night" again. She held her head up and her narrow shoulders pulled back a bit as if she looked the challenge in the face. It sounded a lot less shaky.

"See? Much better." Emma nodded. "We just have to practice a lot. You know what? You can come to my shop and we'll tell your daddy you're helping me with a surprise. He'll think it's a chocolate surprise, but it'll be a singing surprise. Then we can practice all the time."

Casey smiled up at her. "Thank you. You know such good singing tricks. You're so smart." She flung her arms around Emma's waist and hugged her. "Thank you. I love you, Emma."

I love you? When is the last time someone said that to me? I can't remember.

Emma leaned down to return the hug. "I love you too, Casey, you're a very special little girl." Her throat constricted at the idea this precious little girl was leaving from her life again, with her daddy.

Grant will be so happy to see his little girl conquering hurdles and getting more confidence. The look on his face when he sees her on that stage will be priceless. She hugged her tightly. "Now get into bed. Your feet must be freezing."

"Like ice cubes." Casey let go of her and dived into the bed, pulling up her legs and rubbing her toes. "It's better already. I can sing now." Her eyes beamed. "And I can come to your shop. Will you tell Daddy about it?"

"Sure. Now you go to sleep." Emma couldn't resist leaning down and pulling the duvet over Casey. She smiled at her. "Sweet dreams."

Casey pushed her head into the soft pillow and grinned. "Nighty night." She closed her eyes. The soft light from the bedside lamp played across her features. Emma reached out and brushed back her hair.

Casey needs just that little push to trust in herself. And I'll be there for her.

She tiptoed to the door and opened it, slipped out and left it ajar. The paper sunflowers rustled in the draft. She went to the stairs and looked down. In a flash, the sense of depth grabbed her, tipping her world, and she stepped back, her breathing catching in her throat. She closed her eyes a moment to steady her nerves. *It's too steep, I can't do it.*

Of course you can, just take the first step.

A sound came from below, footfalls, and then a hand touched her face and Grant's voice said, "Emma? Are you okay?"

She opened her eyes and looked into his worried expression. He was standing right in front of her, the abyss of the stairs at his back. "Be careful," she said, "the stairs…"

Shut up, they're nothing to him. He climbs them every day.

Grant said, "They're pretty steep. Guests often complain about them. Let me walk ahead of you. Just hold on to the railing tight."

She followed him and once she had taken the first step, it was easier. *See, nothing to it.* Down on solid ground, she didn't know where to look. But Grant smiled at her and brushed her arm a moment. "How was Casey? Up to something, I suppose?"

"Well, it turned out she had a big request." Emma tried to sound innocent. "She wants to help me in the shop with a special surprise. So, if you could drop her off tomorrow morning when you're coming to pick up the deliveries, that would be great."

"Are you sure she won't be any trouble? This is the busiest time of the year for you."

"I like having her around. And her surprise is very special. It's no problem."

"All right then. I'll drop her off." He winked at her. "If I get a little something for my troubles." There was a timbre to Grant's voice, a sort of teasing undertone that spread like fire through her veins. *He's flirting with me.*

What do I say now?

"Tea for Emma," Mrs. Galloway waved at her from the kitchen entrance, holding out a yellow mug with a ladybug pattern. "Come pick a teabag. Or do you want loose leaves?"

Loose leaves? She could barely recall what those were.

Tea, right. With jittery knees she walked over and picked a teabag from the wooden box Mrs. Galloway offered her. "Thanks." She dipped it into the hot water and inhaled the scent. *Liquorice? I thought I chose jasmine.*

She blinked. Grant was turning her world upside down like a ride on a rollercoaster. Nothing was sensible anymore, predictable or safe.

It can only end in heartbreak.

But even that certainty couldn't knock some sense into her silly heart. January would be for picking up the pieces. December was the time to believe in miracles.

Chapter Ten

"There you go, Mr. Winter." Emma gave her large snowman the center spot on her booth's counter. Casey had helped her put the marzipan scarf on. She had also insisted on giving him a name. With suggestions ranging from Blizzard to Crooky because his nose sat at an odd angle, they had laughed so much her cheeks still hurt.

And with every singing session Casey's voice had grown stronger and her confidence in her performance had gone up a notch. *If only Grant had been around more.* He had breezed in and out to pick up deliveries, staying only a few minutes to chat. It always seemed too short.

Last time he had dropped Casey off at the shop, he had been in some kind of a rush to get to an appointment, and as Emma had seen the outfit he wore—the crisp white shirt, neat jacket, gray pants and polished leather shoes—she had suddenly feared that this "appointment" was a job application. After all, if he wanted to leave, he had to be applying for jobs. Looking after him as he had walked away briskly to his car, she had wished with all her heart he wouldn't get the job.

She grimaced. *What kind of friend are you? Be happy for him that he's ready to chase his dreams again.*

Emma's hands trembled as she straightened the boxes with bonbons surrounding Mr. Winter, each decorated with a red ribbon and a mini glittery ornament or tiny glass heart. A silver tray held samples of her new flavors: cherry ganache and coco cream.

At the other booths, locals were busy stacking up their wares. She waved to Cleo, who wore reindeer antlers on her head, and the baker's wife who was carefully building a gingerbread house village on her booth's counter. The tiny church was frosted in white, and sparkly icing created a pond where miniature people were skating.

Everyone seemed to be in the best of moods, humming or singing along with the music coming from the speakers which were hidden here and there among the greenery. On the stage a band was getting everything ready for their live performance. The keyboard player ran his hand lightly across the keys, and the guitar man strummed a few chords.

Small arms hugged her, and Casey stood beside her. She wore a dark blue dress with a red fleece on top. Part of her curls were pulled back and secured with sparkly clasps. "I told Gran about my song," she breathed as Emma leaned over. "She helped me dress up and do my hair. What do you think?" She gestured with both hands along her appearance, pointing at her red boots with snowy white fluffy trimming.

"Super festive. Perfect."

Casey nodded. She fidgeted with her hands. "What if I forget the words?"

"You won't. You know them by heart. Once you've started singing, they'll come. You don't even have to think about it." *The less you think at all, the better. Believe me.*

"But the stage is very big." Casey threw an anxious look in its direction. "And all of those people watching."

"They will think you're very brave to perform for them. It will be all right. Remember what I told you about your posture. Take a deep breath, relax your shoulders. Just imagine you're in the shop with me, singing for Mr. Winter."

Casey giggled. "I will. Thanks for helping me." She hugged Emma again.

Emma held her tightly a moment. "You can do it."

"Hello, Emma." Mrs. Galloway stood a few feet away. Casey said she wanted to say hi to Cleo and darted off to the bookshop booth where her friend put the last red and white candy canes in place among the stacks of books. Cleo sneaked Casey a cane and winked at her, laughing about something.

Mrs. Galloway closed in.

Emma's breath caught. *Maybe she's angry about Casey performing and suspects* you *put her up to it.* She dug her heels into the snow, preparing herself. *Just stay calm.*

"Your booth looks amazing." Mrs. Galloway smiled at her.

"Thank you." Her knees wobbled at the idea that her hostess here at the tree farm wasn't happy with her, and it was Grant's mother too, and Casey's gran. All her plans for a comfy cooking session might go out of the window.

"Casey wants to perform, and I heard you helped her prepare for it," she said.

"Yes, it's a surprise for Grant."

Mrs. Galloway's smile deepened. "This is a big thing for Casey. She hates to be the center of attention, you know. She was so shy and quiet when she came here and now this. I can't believe it's true."

Emma relaxed a little. "She came up with the idea all by herself. I just helped her prepare a little. She already knew the words and the tune; she just needed a bit more…confidence."

Mrs. Galloway nodded. "And you gave that to her. I can't tell you how grateful I am for that."

Emma's stomach squeezed. Mrs. Galloway was grateful now, but what would happen at the actual moment Casey had to perform? She might freeze or feel like she made a fool of herself in front of the entire town. The experience might set her back.

Grant will hate that I helped her do this. The panic swirling in her chest made it difficult for her to breathe deep.

"We all need a little help with confidence sometimes, Emma," Mrs. Galloway said. "Casey had all these thoughts in her head that her mommy had left her for something she had done wrong. It was heartbreaking to see. But she survived. She became stronger. We can't always protect her. We have to let her go make her own decisions and…"

Fall on her face? Everything inside Emma resisted this, but she didn't speak. She couldn't without sounding on the verge of tears.

"I tell myself every day that it will be all right," Mrs. Galloway said. "With Casey and with Grant. I have to believe that." She squeezed Emma's arm lightly. "You can believe it too."

A voice boomed over the speakers announcing that the fair was about to begin. Visitors were pouring in, dressed up warm, and started to explore the offer. *Ooh*s and *aah*s about the booths resounded and the band played the first Christmas song.

The smell of mulled wine and hot chocolate was on the air.

My very first big event representing the shop. And it's not chocolates I'm worried about or making sales. But that little girl on that huge stage.

• • •

"This is even better than last year," an elderly man said and slapped Grant on the shoulder. As he was two heads shorter, the slap landed somewhere on Grant's back.

"Thanks," Grant replied automatically. He was vaguely aware of the Christmas music playing, all the scents, the bustle of the people, the chaos of the fair he remembered from his childhood when his grandparents had had a fair here already. It was such a long-standing family tradition that he couldn't recall a time when it hadn't been there. The skies were clear so the only snow falling was the fine drift swept off the trees by the breeze. People walked hand in hand past the stalls, looking for that perfect Christmas present for loved ones to wrap and put under their tree. A Galloway tree, probably. This was what his family had built in generations of hard work. And he was a part of this.

The song stopped, and the band leader spoke into the microphone, "And now ladies and gentlemen, we have a very special performance. We'll be playing that all-time favorite, that classic, 'Silent Night,' to accompany a sweet little lady who wants to sing for you. Here she is. Casey Galloway."

What? Grant jerked upright upon hearing his daughter's name. *That can't be right.* He stared at the stage, hoping some other kid would appear. But it was his little girl walking up to the band leader and accepting the microphone from him. Casey in her fleece jacket and dress, her cheeks red and her eyes full of apprehension. The tightness of her lips betrayed she was terrified and wanted to be anywhere but on the enormous stage.

No, princess… He wanted to run to the platform, jump onto it and shelter her in his arms, tell her she didn't have to do this.

Casey stood there, very still, staring out across the people. Grant couldn't look away from her face, the tightness in her jaw. *She's paralyzed. She can't get a word out. Do something, anything, to spare her this.*

The band already started playing the intro. The leader was counting down to give Casey the signal to start.

Something stirred in the corner of his eye. Emma abandoned her stall and made her way to the front of the crowd at the stage. She lifted both her hands and made a heart gesture at Casey. Casey didn't seem to see her at first, but then her eyes lit in recognition and her whole face relaxed in a dazzling smile.

The leader pointed at her, and she began singing. Her voice was high and pure. Grant stared at his little girl, rooted to the ground. *I never knew she could sing like that.*

People elbowed each other and exchanged excited looks but no one spoke as if they knew this song needed silence.

Casey's voice was soft on the first few lines but then rose in strength, filling the area. An elderly lady close to Grant wiped a tear away. Her husband put an arm around her. Grant looked at Emma, who was beaming at Casey. He wanted to wrap his arm around her and tell her that whatever she had done to his little girl to make her confident like this, he would be forever grateful to her for it. But she was too far away for him to wrestle his way over to her and he didn't want to disturb his daughter's concentration.

Casey was on the last lines and people started to sing along, at first hesitantly then stronger until it was like a full choir of voices, young and old, strong and weak, high and low, singing the season's joy.

When the last note died down, everybody stood a moment, breathing the chill winter air, listening as it were to the music drifting away to heaven above. Then they broke into life, clapping and cheering. Casey turned bright red and fumbled with the microphone, but her eyes beamed. Emma pushed to the stage and Casey ran over and jumped into her arms. Emma hugged her tightly.

Grant grinned. *That's one special woman.*

His phone buzzed in his pocket. *Not now.*

It kept going, like an alarm beeping in the cockpit, warning him something was up.

Okay then. He pulled it up and checked the screen. *Ivo?* He hadn't talked to his old buddy in ages. He took a few steps away and answered, holding the phone close to his ear.

"Hello, Grant. I got great news for you. I found you the perfect job."

"Job?" he repeated, not sure he had heard right.

"Yes. It's in the Florida Keys. You'll be based on one of the islands and fly out to the others. It's a day job where you determine your own hours so perfect to take care of your little girl too. And she will love it there. Dolphins, turtles, flamingos. You can raise her away from the city, out where everything is still wild and free. Perfect for you, buddy. How about it? I can put in a word for you. Guy who runs the air shuttle service is married to a friend of my sister's. That's how I heard."

Grant's mind whirled with images of the Florida Keys, white beaches, palm trees, wildlife, boating, raising his little girl in such a beautiful environment, being able to fly again and still have enough time for her. It sounded like the dream offer. And at the same time he saw Casey, standing on her own feet again, beside Emma, looking up at her with an adoring smile, and his gut clenched. Locals came up to her to tell her how well she had done, and she didn't hide away but talked to them, gesturing and laughing.

How do you tell her you're taking her away from her new friends?

He clutched the phone. Something about leaving seemed intuitively wrong. But maybe he had become overprotective. If it had been up to him, she'd never have gone up on that stage. *But she could do that, and she can also make new friends in Florida. She'll be so excited to see flamingos, go out on a boat. Open up the world to her, one step at a time. It'll be one big adventure.*

"Grant?" Ivo's voice echoed in his ear. "Are you there?"

"Yes, thanks for the offer, sounds great. I'm at a Christmas fair so I can't talk. Can I call you back?"

"What is there to call me back about? This is the perfect offer."

Grant recalled all the applications he had sent out and all the rejections, or the deep silence, he had gotten in return. Yes, this could be it. His need for regular hours didn't make him the flexible candidate most employers liked to see. He should jump at the chance.

"I'll put in a word for you," Ivo repeated. "I'm sure they'll take you on. Happy to help you. You're a born pilot. Bye."

Grant lowered his phone and lifted his face to the skies. This time he wouldn't be flying away from Casey anymore. He'd be near her all the time. They could even fly together, go on daytrips to islands. Share his love of the great outdoors with his daughter.

"Daddy!" Little arms hugged his waist. He looked down at Casey grinning up at him. "Did you hear me sing?"

"You were amazing. I'm so proud of you." He slipped the phone into his pocket and lifted her in his arms. She hugged his neck and rubbed her warm cheek against his. He expected Emma to be hard on her heels and wanted to tell her how much he had loved that song. But she wasn't there.

Half turning, he spotted her behind her booth, selling bonbon boxes to eager customers. *Of course. She's here for her business.*

The voice over the PA invited the mayor to come to the stage now and announce which three wishes from the Christmas tree at the community center would be granted. The town father, bundled up in a thick coat and a red scarf, climbed the steps and waved at the crowd. He was carrying three cards in his hand and people were squeezing each other's arm in excitement, hoping that their wish had made it.

Grant had no idea what kind of things people might wish for, but the ones granted had to be within the city council's power and budget to fulfill. New cars or cruises wouldn't be eligible.

The mayor grabbed the microphone and cleared his throat. "Dear townspeople, friends..." He smiled. "I have here three wonderful wishes we're going to make come true. Things people asked for, not for themselves but for others. A friend, a neighbor or the community. I'm always pleased with the kindness and spirit of togetherness displayed in the wishes hung in our community center's tree. And this year it was particularly hard to choose which wishes we were going to fulfill. So many were selfless and touching."

Grant glanced at Emma's booth. She was listening to the mayor with keen attention, her eyes alight in her warm face. *Did anyone make a wish for her? To give her something special...*

"First up," the mayor said, "we have this wish." He held up the card. "A patron of the library who wants to remain anonymous is asking us for the budget to create a service where books can be delivered to those who are not able to visit the library in person. This is particularly pressing in this time of year where snow can keep the elderly homebound. A beautiful idea."

He held up another card. "A suggestion that the town could provide meals to those who are not able to cook fresh for themselves every day. And..."

He showed the third card. "A wish for a project at the community center where those who have no family can eat together.

"Now the council and I decided it would be a great idea to combine these three wishes into a single project. One night a week volunteers will be cooking at the community center. Those who want to eat together can go there for a free meal. Those who are unable to come will have their meal delivered to their home, along with books of their choosing.

"The librarian and her volunteers have already agreed to take people's orders for books on that day. They'll be ready in reusable totes, for the meal volunteers to pick up and take along to the addresses they are delivering to. Meal volunteers will come from the already existing cooking class at the community center and you can also sign up at the community center booth on the fairgrounds if you want to get involved. Aside from volunteers, we're looking for shopkeepers who want to donate food or other items to the project. Let's make this amazing together."

Cheers and applause welcomed this new venture. Emma was beaming, and Grant figured she'd join in for sure, donating bonbons for after dinner coffee, or as a volunteer, cooking or delivering the meals and books to the elderly.

Too bad he was leaving and couldn't be a part of it, too.

But the Floridian job offer was the perfect chance to build a solid future for himself and Casey. Everything Ivo had told him about it was exactly right for his situation.

Like a wish granted, although he hadn't put it in the Christmas tree.

He should be dancing around the fairgrounds with his daughter, to celebrate he had actually done it. Secured that amazing future for the both of them. *Why am I not feeling it?*

No sense of peace descended on him, no conviction it was all right what he was doing. Just unrest crawling across his nerve ends, something off radar he couldn't pin down.

If there was one thing he had learned on his climbing trips, it was to trust his gut. It knew trouble was coming long before any factual signs of bad weather or unstable rocks showed. Might even have saved his life on several occasions.

Right now, that interfering gut was whispering at him he was making a huge mistake. But this was one time he wasn't going to listen. Because listening might mean taking a lot more risk than just accepting things at face value.

Chapter Eleven

"You don't have to buy chocolates from me," Emma said as she carried the boxes into the kitchen. It was two days after the Christmas fair, and she had worked from the moment she rolled out of bed until she could fall into it at night. Her back twinged with every move and her eyelids pricked as if sand had been blown into them. She suppressed a yawn.

Mrs. Galloway waved a hand. "We're entertaining a ton of people after the Christmas morning service and I want something special for them. Thanks so much for making these." She flipped the lid and studied the little trees that all had tiny ornament decorations of colorful frosting. "You must have spent some time on them."

"I love special assignments." Emma stretched herself and rolled back her shoulders. The exhaustion of her long to-do list seeped through her every fiber and these moments in the carefree atmosphere of the Galloway tree farm provided the breather she had been aching for.

It didn't matter where Grant was and if she'd even see him now that she was here. She had made friends with his entire family, not just him. He had seemed different at the fair. After Casey had sung. Like he wasn't happy with it. There had been something in his eyes, a bit pensive, faraway. *As if he'd already left Wood Creek mentally.* And instead of coming in person to help with the deliveries, he had sent his father along. What was he up to?

None of your business. He already gave you a lot of his time. He doesn't owe you any more. She shook herself up and forced a smile at Mrs. Galloway, who was still admiring the detailing on the chocolate trees. "I've got coffee ready," her hostess said. "Would you find Fay? She's in the big barn."

"Sure." Emma stepped out of the back door and made her way through the fresh snow to the big barn. It seemed like a normal thing to do, as if she had been coming here for years. Everybody was so welcoming, kind and relaxed. They had a busy company to run but they did it together, with warmth and caring. She hadn't yet heard them yell at each other or act snappy and irritated. No doubt it did happen at times, after all, they were humans like everybody else, but there was a decided kindness here, a good heart.

The tension in her tired shoulders seeped away, and Emma smiled as she pushed open the door into the big barn. The invigorating smell of the trees was almost like a welcoming touch on her face. She inhaled it deep into her and looked around, drinking in all details. On the work bench against the wall big ledgers sat, in leather bands, and tools alternated with dirty mugs which nobody bothered to ever take inside for a wash. On the wall an old handsaw hung, a bit rusty, representing the old days before power saws had come upon the scene. This was a place she would love to wander through, touching a tree branch here and there, just being a part of it.

But she had to find Fay and bring her in for coffee. Mrs. Galloway would be pouring it into mugs by now and getting cookies ready.

Stamping her cold feet, Emma walked around quickly, peeking about her. Nobody in sight. Her breath formed clouds in the cold air. In here there was no heating. *Oh, there!* At the far end Fay stood at a rickety table, leaning over a red wrapped something on the table. Her hands rested on the edge. Emma drew near, about to call out for her.

But wait. What's that? Fay's shoulders were shaking. Smothered sounds broke the silence.

Emma froze, her one hand coming up to her face in shock. *This is awkward. She wants to be alone.* Her stomach squeezed. *Please, no, nothing terrible hitting the happy Galloway family. Not again.* The death of Grant's wife had been enough.

She went over and stood beside the other woman. "Are you all right?" she asked softly.

Fay jerked upright and stared at her through wet lashes. "Emma. I had no idea you were here." She wiped her eyes. "I'm sorry. I just lost it for a moment. It's Christmas stress." She swallowed hard.

"If you want to talk about it, I'll listen." Emma put a hand on her arm. "And I can keep a secret."

"Thanks." Fay looked at her with a hesitant smile. "It's the whole thing with Grant. I just…"

Grant? What about him?

Fay knotted her fingers. "Last year, he wasn't even here for Christmas. He had accepted a call for help from a friend who had to take a plane out to Asia and couldn't go at the last moment. Grant flew it out for him. I was just… I didn't understand. I mean, Christmas is the time of year to be home, with family. Especially if you have a daughter who's still upset about her mommy going away. But Grant wasn't here and— this year I thought it was all different. He seemed different. More mellow and relaxed. No longer chopping down trees like a madman, you know. And then we find out he's taking a job in Florida." Her voice wobbled on the name as if she could barely wrench it out.

Florida? The floor shifted under Emma's feet. *So far away? I thought, I hoped—*

"I guess I shouldn't even know." Fay wiped her eyes again and gave Emma a defiant look. "I was curious, you know, what Grant was doing at night in the workroom upstairs. I just felt like he was up to something. I didn't mean to pry. I was just in the landing to put away the laundry and I heard his voice. I guessed he was on the phone, so I walked over and listened at the door."

She hung her head, knotting her fingers again. "I know it was bad, but I just couldn't help myself. It happened before I really knew what I was doing. I was standing at the door, listening in, and I overheard him talking to someone about a job in Florida, flying tourists from island to island. The Keys, you know. He was discussing all the details. Where he might live, if there was a good school there for Casey."

The tiredness that had just been an undercurrent in her veins now hit her like a ton of bricks, pushing all air out of her. Grant leaving, for Florida, taking Casey with him. Islands, sunshine, wildlife, of course it sounded amazing. Especially to an adventurer like him. *That's why he hasn't come by the shop. He's busy getting everything set up for his move.*

"He didn't even tell us he was looking for a job again. Or maybe he did mention it, but I hoped—" Fay swallowed hard. "I thought that it would be difficult for him to find one."

She sniffed. "I hoped he wouldn't find work as a pilot anymore and stay around Wood Creek. I like having him and Casey here. It will be so quiet without them." She sobbed again, hiding her face in her hands.

Emma clenched her hands into fists by her side. In a situation like this her first impulse was to say something to cheer Fay up. But her throat was too tight to get out any upbeat words. Any words at all. Grant's expression came to mind as he had talked about flying, being weightless, being free. He needed that. They had to let him go.

"Sorry about this." Fay straightened up and drew a shuddering breath. "I don't want to spoil your festive mood." Her features contorted as she pointed at the red wrapped object on the table. "This is for you. Grant promised you a Christmas piece, right?"

Emma nodded. That first time he had come to her shop. Why had she agreed to his offer to spend some time with his daughter? *You should have known better. It's always like this. Connect, say goodbye. Over and over.*

"Grant and Casey made it for you the other day," Fay said, "so when Mom told me that you were bringing the chocolates, I wanted to take it in, and they can give it to you. I didn't mean to have a breakdown like this." She forced a smile, but her features contorted as she fought new tears.

"It's okay. I understand how you feel." Emma wrapped an arm around Fay and patted her shoulder. *I understand better than you know.*

"Thanks." Fay smiled at her through her tears.

"Your mother's got coffee ready. We should go."

"You're right. I don't want her to see me crying." Fay rubbed her face with both of her hands, just making the blotting worse. "We can't have that, can we? I'm not supposed to know anything yet and Grant won't tell before Christmas, I guess. To make it easier on Mom and Dad. It would break their hearts and ruin the holidays. It will be our last time together like this." She exhaled in a huff. "Just listen to me sounding morbid. I'm too sentimental about it, I know. We can call all the time. Maybe next year they'll come over and stay with us for the holidays. Who knows?"

Emma's heart missed a beat thinking of Grant,

sunburned from all the island sunshine, Casey being a year older, turning a bit lanky maybe, and a woman with them, someone Grant had met out there, who could be a mother to Casey. Her stomach plummeted. *No, please.*

"They will come and visit," Fay said in a tone as if she had to convince herself. "But it won't be the same. I hate change. I just want things to stay the way they are."

If only they could.

Fay extracted a tissue and blew her nose. "I was already sneezing this morning so if my mother asks about my red eyes, I'll just say it's the cold, okay? I'll carry this." She picked up the red wrapped present.

"Fine with me." Emma followed Fay out of the barn and back to the house. *Act normal*, she repeated to herself with every step.

Mrs. Galloway was busy putting a cookie jar on the table where the mugs and coffee pot were already in place. "At last," she said without looking at them. "I thought I had to come out and find you." She straightened up and smiled at Emma. "Sit down." She glanced at Fay and her eyes narrowed as if she was onto something.

But she didn't say anything. She just went back to the sink to fetch a pitcher with fresh milk for the coffee and then they sat down, cradling their hot mugs and chatting about the fair and how much everyone had enjoyed themselves. Emma's gaze kept returning to the present that sat in the middle of the table. *Don't cry when unwrapping it. Don't cry.*

Just as Emma was half into a muddled story about a fair she had visited as a child, the back door opened and Casey burst in, her coat full of snow. She ran to Mrs. Galloway and hid behind her. "Daddy wants to throw snow all over me," she giggled.

Grant rushed in with two gloved hands full of snow. He skidded to a halt and looked about him as if he had no idea where Casey was.

Emma stared at him, the snow on the shearling collar of his leather jacket, the smile on his suntanned face, the teasing look in his deep brown eyes. He was just perfect. And he was leaving town. She looked down and blew into her coffee although it wasn't hot anymore.

Casey laughed and ran around the table, scooting into the bench and sitting beside Emma. "I'm safe here, Daddy."

"Don't count on it."

Emma glanced up and his eyes were on her. He lifted his hands full of snow a bit higher as if challenging her. What would be like being out in the snow with him, him coming over to throw snow at her, rubbing it across her cheeks? Laughing and pushing each other and then falling against him and his strong arms wrapping around her and holding her.

She blinked. *Stop fantasizing like that. It isn't real. Real is the Floridian job offer. He can never be yours.*

• • •

Grant looked away from Emma. The carefree mood that had rushed through his system during the snow fight with Casey evaporated, and alertness sharpened his senses like when a cockpit meter gave an unusual reading.

He didn't know what had happened with Emma, but, somehow, she had changed. A spark that had been there before was missing. He wanted to unearth the cause, but he had no manual listing possible problems and their solutions.

He went to the back door and tossed out the snow, then pulled his gloves off and threw them on the sink.

His mother clicked her tongue, but he ignored her, peeling his coat off and swinging that over a chair. He filled a mug with coffee for himself. Casey said, "We made you a present." Wrapping paper rustled as she leaned over the table to pull it toward her. "Careful," he warned. "It's heavy."

"I love that paper," Emma said. "You can make roses from it."

"Show me." Casey leaned against her.

Emma touched the present gingerly as if she was afraid to break it. She tore off a bit of paper and divided it into three squares, putting them on top of one another, and then with one swift movement turned them into a small flower. "There you go." She gave it to Casey.

"How did you do that? Show me again."

"Let Emma unwrap the present first." His mother took the flower from Casey's hand and stuck it in her hair.

"Daddy said you didn't have a tree," Casey said. "Or room for one. But you can put this anywhere. I made the star for on top."

Emma's features relaxed in a smile as she scanned the single branch put upright in the pot like a little tree, decorated with golden bows and a glittery star on top. Casey had painted and cut it herself, leaving it a bit uneven. But Emma said it was perfect and hugged Casey.

He had meant to say something casual like, "That is what I call a custom-made piece," but the words wouldn't come. The unrest that had toured his system since the fair grew into a storm.

"I'll show you what I made in school," Casey said. "It's in my room." She ran off upstairs. The paper flower flew from her hair and landed on the floor.

His mother rose and said she had laundry to finish in the attic. "Lend me a hand, will you, Fay?"

"Sure." Fay jumped to her feet and followed his mother.

A deep silence descended on the kitchen. Emma sat with her hands wrapped around her coffee mug, her gaze on the table. Her hair, which hung loose around her warm face, curled a little.

His hand itched to brush the hair away, tuck it behind her ear and ask her what she was thinking about. He went to pick up the paper rose and stood staring at it as it rested on his palm. He turned to her, his mind still grappling for the right thing to say. She eyed him, with a slight frown.

"What?" they both asked at the same time.

She burst out laughing. The sparks in her eyes lit up again. *Good.*

"I was just thinking"—she gestured with a hand—"how glad I am it's almost Christmas and I can take a few days off."

"We're all looking forward to that." *Lame. So general and unpersonal. You can do better than that.*

"Really?" Emma studied him with a frown. "I thought you didn't like Christmas? Fay told me you weren't here last year. Flying to Asia?"

"Just helping a friend." He hesitated and then sat down opposite her. "But you're right, I was glad to have an excuse to get away. Christmas is a time of togetherness, peace, joy. I wasn't feeling any of those things."

"But being away from home, in a city of millions, sitting alone in a hotel room, you can't have felt much better."

He scoffed. "You're right about that. Wherever I went, the situation was the same. I missed Lily, Casey's carefree laughter, the past. Most of all, how I never appreciated what I had."

Emma tilted her head as if probing his remark. "Did you feel guilty?"

Got it in one. Still, he wasn't about to tell all. He shrugged. "I guess. I had been away so often. It was something Lily and I agreed on. She had her studio, her art, the exhibitions, and Casey. I had my job, my climbing trips with pals. Lots of my friends did it the same way." *Lousy excuses.*

He wanted to leave it at that, but somehow the words

just kept coming. "When I was at home, I loved spending time with my family. But I also took off again, just like that. I can't imagine now being away from Casey for even a day. Back then it was easy to go for weeks on end." He shook his head trying to remember how he'd done it. "Somehow I never realized how...things can be over before you know it."

• • •

Emma's hand tensed, ready to reach across the table and cover his. *Don't say you understand. How could you? Losing your parents isn't the same as losing your partner.*

Grant said, "In the past I made a lot of choices I'm not proud of anymore. I feel like I should have been a better dad. I promised myself I'd change it all around. Yeah, sure." He laughed ruefully. "Even when I'm trying, I don't know how I'm doing, really. If I know what she needs."

"You're a great dad. She loves you."

"Sure, she even loved me last year when I left right before Christmas. It was the most selfish thing, but I just had to be far away where nobody knew me and would wonder how I was doing. It was all about me."

"That's not true. I bet you also went away because you knew she'd feel how sad you were, and you didn't want to ruin Christmas for her."

"Maybe. But you know what? I came back from that trip and she ran for me and jumped into my arms." Pushing back his chair with a jerk, he got to his feet and paced the kitchen. "That can't be right."

The frustration in his footfalls beat through her. But he was looking at it from the wrong angle. "That's what love is about, isn't it? That you don't need to earn it."

"Don't you think I was a bad father leaving her like that when she needed me most? Come on, you can say it."

She shook her head. "We're not discussing whether you were a bad father last Christmas. You just told me you weren't there enough, and she still loved you. Isn't that reassuring? That she will still love you even if you make mistakes? Believe me, kids don't want perfect parents. They just want parents, period."

He halted as if stopped short. "I'm sorry. I wasn't thinking how this whole discussion is for you."

"That's not important." Emma waved a hand. "Casey came to my shop to make *you* happy. You're the center of her world. As long as she has you, she will be all right. Trust me."

Grant stood tight as if ready to deny it all, then he relaxed with a sigh. His expression changed from cold and doubtful to warm and assured in a heartbeat. "You always seem to know the exact right thing to say. Thanks, Emma."

Her heartbeat stuttered and she had to struggle to breathe normally. The warmth in his face reeled her in. *Brush those worry lines away. Put your hand on his chest and tell him he has a good heart and will always make the right decisions for his daughter.*

But that heart had decided the two of them were leaving town. That heart was going after a new adventure, the big open skies. And she was staying behind, with her little shop and her newfound hometown, the beginning of roots she wanted to plant firmly here into this New Hampshire soil.

"Here they are!" Casey came in, carefully carrying two colorful objects. She put them on the table and ran a loving finger across. Made of clay, they were two puppies, one painted black and white with a crooked red collar, the other brown with a blue collar. "What do you think?"

"They're adorable. Do they have names?"

"Spot and Muffin. Bob said the brown looks like muffin dough." Casey beamed. "Do you want one?"

"But you made them. And shouldn't they be together?"

"I want you to have Muffin. He can watch over you while you're sleeping." Casey pushed the brown dog over to her.

That cute little dog would be the last thing she saw when turning off the light, the first thing when she got out of bed in the morning. In her living room the mini tree with Casey's star would sit on the table or in the windowsill. Little touches making her apartment a real home.

"Thanks." She gave Casey a hug. Looking up, she caught Grant's eye. He stood there as if he was waiting for her to come over and hug him as well. *Nonsense. You just gave him some friendly advice. Be smart, keep your distance. He'll be gone soon enough.*

Chapter Twelve

Grant lowered his little girl into bed and smiled down at her. "Ready for sweet dreams?" He was still riding on a wave of reassurance that he would do good with Casey. Maybe his doubts had been weighing heavier on his mind than he had realized. But opening up to Emma had been easy and her advice priceless. *She's special in every way.*

He sat down on the edge of the bed and folded his hands around Casey's hands so she could say her bedtime prayers. Watching her face as she prayed, her eyes closed tightly and her lashes trembling on her cheeks, tenderness crashed his chest. She was vulnerable and small, but also brave and far bigger than he wanted her to be. He wanted her to stay little always, hiding in his arms, against his heart.

"And make Emma happy too," Casey prayed. "Amen."

Breath escaped him as if someone had punched him in the gut. "Don't you think Emma is happy?"

"Emma is all alone." Casey nodded at him. "She doesn't have a family and she doesn't have a dog. I would like a dog."

"You've got Spot." He pointed to the clay creation on her

nightstand.

"A real one." She sat up and leaned over, leaning her head against his shoulder. "Can I have a dog, Daddy? Just a very small puppy. He won't eat much."

Getting a dog just as they were moving away would be a terrible idea, but he didn't want to tell his daughter about the changes just yet. Not talking about it made it less real. Almost like an idea he could still bin. But that friend of Ivo's on the island had mailed him about his daughter's school which might also be perfect for Casey and included the contact information for a real estate agent who could pitch him some available houses. Smooth sailing. And still he kept scanning for the snag.

Hoping for the snag even?

"Can I have a puppy, Daddy? Pleaaase?" Casey pressed herself against him, putting on her most pleading voice.

"I don't know, sweetie. Dogs aren't goldfish. They need a lot of care." He peeled her away from him. "It's time to sleep now."

"I asked Santa for a puppy." Casey beamed at him. "Maybe he will bring one."

Grant already knew "Santa" would be smarter than that but didn't want to ruin his daughter's excitement. "Who knows?" He kissed her on the cheek. "Now sleep."

"Where's the golden bird?" Casey asked. He thought she was already sleepy and not making sense. "We had a golden bird back home in the Christmas tree."

In a flash, he was back at that last Christmas together in their suburban home. The tree dominated the room, all dressed up with ornaments and bows and glittering lights. Lily's doing of course. While she put the last decorations in place, Casey had run around the tree, pointing out how much space there was underneath for all of the presents.

Those decorations. He had packed them up with so many

other boxes from their home when he had sold it off because he couldn't bear to live there any longer. The boxes had come with him from Chicago, were shoved into the attic here. To look at later, when he thought he was ready for it. And there they had sat until now. Untouched.

Casey made a soft sighing sound. Her eyes were already closed, and it seemed she was drifting into sleep already. No wonder after their wild snowball fight.

He brushed her forehead with a grin. He'd go up and look for the golden bird and the other decorations. Maybe he could even bring in a small pine and they would decorate their very own tree. It could be in another corner of the living room. Mom and Dad were surrounded by trees, one more wouldn't matter to them. *Casey's Christmas surprise. Can't wait to see her face.*

· · ·

Emma accompanied the elderly woman to the door of her shop and smiled at her. "Thank you very much. I hope your grandkids love the chocolates. And merry Christmas."

"Thank you. I'm really looking forward to seeing them again. It has been ages. Merry Christmas to you." She made her way gingerly across the frozen snow, the bag with her purchases on her arm.

The smile on Emma's face faded away. Christmas had been her lifelong enemy, everyone talking about who they were going to spend it with, what fun it would be. She had longed for January when her life didn't feel quite so empty. But this year she actually had a place to go to and people who would be happy to see her.

People she longed to be with for a whole night of food, games and some early presents. Her teapot for Mrs. Galloway was bought and wrapped up.

But every time she saw it sitting beside the couch, her breath caught as if she was standing on top of a ladder knowing she could plunge down. *It isn't safe at all.*

It hadn't been from the start. She had known it and still she had pushed on. Seeing Grant more often, agreeing to Casey's singing scheme. Oh, there had been enough solid reasons. Just helping out, making friends in her new town. But her heart didn't buy into the friends thing. It wanted more.

If only Grant would stay around town a few months longer. *No, it's good this way. You would have given yourself away.* Maybe she already had?

Grant had shot her a few probing looks. Like he wanted to read her thoughts. *Good thing he can't.*

Or did she even want to? He was going to leave. It might be her only chance to...

To do what? He wants to go, and you have to stay here. For the shop. She stared at her counter full of chocolates, the little Christmas tree on top, the gold and silver decorations strung along the shelves. Everything she had prepared with love and joy. Her lease of the building ran for four years. Signing those papers had provided the stability she had longed for.

But there was more to life than work. Grant had showed her that. It had been so easy to let her guard down and talk about things she never mentioned to anyone. He and his daughter had been inside her heart before she had known it. She didn't want to fight it. *Just give into it, enjoy the ride while you can.*

The phone rang and she rushed to answer it, grabbing a pad to write the order on.

She tried to listen to the customer describing the bonbons she wanted. But Grant's face kept intruding, his smile, the little changes in his expression when he listened attentively or was focused on something. His roaring laughter resounded around her, and her cheek tingled under the memory of his hand brushing her face, securing the strap of the helmet under her chin.

Just like Grant to make sure you're safe. It's his instinct, nothing more.

I love you, Emma. She pressed the pencil down on the paper so hard the tip broke. Those words she wanted to hear, over and over. *Kids love one thing one day and another the next. Casey will forget you, make new friends in the place she's going to live.*

Emma blinked against the burn behind her eyes. She had better steel herself or she wouldn't be able to make it through Christmas Eve with the Galloways without crying. And she didn't want to draw attention. She had to be strong. Smile even though inside she felt like everything was over.

· · ·

"Are your eyes shut tightly?" Grant asked, leaning over to his daughter to study her closely. She giggled but nodded. "Really tight, Daddy."

He held his hands behind his back, the golden bird in them. The one she had asked about. Going up into the attic, his enthusiasm had been tinged with dread at facing the things he had put away after his wife's death for the first time, but it hadn't hurt as much as he had expected it to. Lily's system had even made him smile, the felt-tip markings on all the boxes leading him straight to the Christmas ones. She had always been organized, something at odds with the image people had of artists as chaotic.

To be able to unearth the decorations without having to touch all the other stuff had been a gift from her to him.

And standing there for a moment, thinking of his earlier life, and of what it had become right now, a reluctant conclusion had darted through his mind: that he wasn't a disaster as a single father after all.

Sure, he made mistakes, but he also knew how to get through to his daughter when she was angry or sad. He knew how to be with her without even saying a word. He knew how to help her when she was afraid, simply by giving her a hug. He was there for her; in ways he had never been before.

And Casey had grown so much from a sad, shy little girl into a beaming, eager, and curious girl who looked at the world with wide open eyes. He could still hear her singing at the fair. That had been amazing. All because of Emma too.

"Daddy, what are you waiting for?" Casey sounded impatient.

"Right. Hold out your hands. Open, palms up."

Casey stretched out her hands and opened them, expectation trembling in her entire tight posture.

Grant produced the golden bird from behind his back and held it out to her. Gently he placed it in her hands. "Now you can look."

Casey snapped her eyes open. She stared a moment, then gasped. "It's the golden bird. You found it. I thought it was gone." She held it to her face and pressed a kiss on it.

"It's all still here." He stepped aside so she could see the table in the back of the room on which he had placed the boxes with Christmas decorations from the attic.

Casey gasped again and ran over. "Oh, the crown with the glitter. And the snow heart. And the other birds with the fluffy tails." She swung around, her eyes alight. "Can we put them on the tree?"

"Even better. I cut off a tree for the both of us. Our tree."

"Our tree," Casey repeated. She smiled a wide, almost disbelieving smile. "Can we decorate it together?"

"That's the idea."

Casey danced through the room with the golden bird clutched in her hands. She stopped and asked breathlessly,

"Can we do it now? Do you have the tree?"

"Yes, it's outside, waiting for you. Go and see."

Casey whooped and ran to the door, returned to put the bird tenderly down in the tissue paper inside one of the boxes. Then she rushed outside.

Grant followed her, his heartbeat racing. Casey stood at the tree he had leaned against the house. It wasn't big, but it was meant for her to be able to reach up to the top and decorate. There was a haze of fresh snow on it and Casey brushed it off the branches.

"You can come live with us now, tree. You will be very pretty. I'll give you a very special name. Like I did for Mr. Winter. He liked his name a lot. I could tell by his nose. It wiggles when he's happy." She looked up at Grant. "Can Emma come and help us decorate?"

Grant blinked at the sudden suggestion. Or was it the breathless rush through his veins, saying, *yes, Emma, of course she has to be here, let's go get her*?

He reached up and rubbed his face a moment as if he was undecided, stalling for time.

"Please?" Casey hung on his arm. "It won't be the same without her."

"Okay." He checked his watch. "I can ask her when she might be free to come over to us. She does have a shop, you know, she can't just leave whenever she wants to."

He could of course call her, but he had to go into town anyway to deliver a few last-minute Christmas cards to the post office. They'd never reach the recipients in time, but his mother had insisted on writing them anyway.

Grant grinned to himself. He leaned over and tapped Casey on her nose. "I'll go and ask her. You look through the boxes and make a plan for the tree, okay?"

"Yes, I'll make a drawing of what has to go where."

Every inch my little girl. Nothing ever works without a plan.

Chapter Thirteen

"Merry Christmas to you too." Grant waved back at the post office clerk before stepping out of the sliding doors back into the chill of new snow. The flakes whirled around him and he could barely see the other side of the street. He turned up his collar and stood a moment, inhaling the cold and rubbing his hands, before sticking them into his pockets and hurrying along the shops with their festively dressed windows. He walked faster as he came closer to Heart Street, his heart skipping a beat every few paces. A sign on the sidewalk blocked his path, reading: *Perfect Christmas gifts: charms.* The red arrow above pointed at the jewelry shop to his right.

Charms?

He studied the pictured examples of a gingerbread house, a sleigh and a Santa. *It'll have to be a Christmas tree. A memento of her first fair and first Christmas in Wood Creek.*

He had never set foot in Wood Creek's jewelry shop so far, but now he gave the family-owned business an appreciative once-over as he stepped inside: nice display windows with fake snow pasted to the glass and a luxurious Christmas wreath on the door, probably bought at the tree farm.

"Hello, Grant." Mrs. Rivers smiled at him. "Can I help you?"

"I'd like a Christmas tree charm. It's a present."

"Oh, for Casey? How sweet. We have several options." She reached under the counter and presented him with a tray decked with blue velvet and a ton of charms attached to it. Dogs and swans and Eiffel towers. *I had no idea there were so many.*

She pointed at the bottom row. "We have Christmas trees in silver and gold. With tiny gemstones too, for ornaments."

Emma's charms were all plain silver. *I don't want her to think I'm showing off. Just a small gift.* "A silver one will be fine. That one with the white top maybe?"

"That's enamel representing snow. Such a cute touch." She took it off. "Do you want us to attach it to the charm bracelet?" She eyed him expectantly as if he could produce said bracelet.

She thinks it's for Casey so… "I don't have it on me. I saw your sign in passing and just stepped in."

"No problem. You can do it later." She put the tiny tree in a black box and wrapped it in paper with candy canes.

A gold-rimmed mirror on the counter reflected his face. He reached up and rubbed his jaw. *Stubble. You should have shaved.*

He raked a hand through his hair to model it. A few gray hairs here and there. He wasn't twenty-five anymore, and it showed.

Yeah, since when has that bothered you?

"That's eighteen dollars, please."

He dug out his wallet and paid.

She put the colorful package in his hand. "Merry Christmas to Casey."

He muttered a goodbye and left the shop, clenching the wrapped box in his hand. The corners cut into his palm through the wrapping paper. He had looked at himself through another's eyes. Emma's eyes. Did she think he was old?

Emma, with her dimples and loose hair and soft hands and…

He had checked himself out in the mirror as if he was sixteen again and going on a date. Inviting the girl he liked to a trip to the movies or a spin in his father's car. *What is this? What's happening to me?*

He looked down at the package in his hand. A gift, right, a small thing, between friends. *Friends?*

Who had he been kidding? There was this warmth when they touched, this protectiveness he felt when people weren't nice to her. The tenderness that swept over him when he had seen her making the heart gesture to his daughter. After all she had done for them, it was logical he wanted to give back to her, right? But it wasn't that straightforward. His gut had been telling him ever since the fair.

Even before that. When she had almost fallen, and he had locked her in his arms. He hadn't wanted to let go again.

Could he actually be… *Uh? No. That is not happening.*

Grant stared at the box, holding the charm as if it had become a ball of fire. No, he wasn't doing that. No feelings, no risks, no complications. Nothing potentially dangerous. He was just building his new life, trying to be a decent dad, finding a job.

You accepted a job, in Florida. You're leaving Wood Creek. Emma is staying. She made that clear.

She wanted stability now after all the forced changes in her life. Plane rides had never meant freedom to her but uprooting, disorientation, having to start over, again and again. His dream was her nightmare. They couldn't be together not even if he wanted to.

And he didn't. He had everything worked out to a T. A job where he could work and still care for Casey. A beautiful place to live, wildlife to explore. A dream come true for the two of them. He had to focus on Casey. On their life together. Nothing more.

He turned away from Heart Street and hurried back to his car. He'd tell Casey that Emma was too busy with her shop to come help decorate the tree. It would be a lie and he did hope Emma wouldn't find out about it later.

I can't do this. It beat through his brain in the rhythm of his rushed footfalls. *I can't watch her smile at Casey and reach out and put the golden bird in place.*

Grant dived into his car and gripped the wheel so tightly his hands hurt. He tried to squeeze some reality into his foolish heart. There was no time for tenderness, there was no room for feelings. He had to stick to his plan.

He turned the ignition on and drove off, putting distance between him and Heart Street where Emma worked hard over her chocolates in her little shop.

He had to prepare himself for facing her again on Christmas Eve. She was invited to spend time with his family so he couldn't tell her she couldn't come. It would be rude, and she didn't deserve that. She had been so sweet to all of them. Casey loved her.

For Casey's sake he would just be kind to her, nice, friendly. He would make sure he didn't sit next to her so their arms couldn't accidentally touch. He would make sure he didn't look at her too often and couldn't embed in his memory how she talked and smiled and…

No. He absolutely wouldn't think about her race across the snow to build snow dogs.

The light on her face when they had lit the lanterns, his arm around her shoulders.

No. January normality was right around the corner. He'd be diving into the move and all those distracting emotions would fade away. *I just have to get through the holidays.*

Chapter Fourteen

Emma stepped out of the car clutching the paper bag holding the wrapped teapot for Mrs. Galloway. With her free hand she smoothed her dress down. The fabric was cool under her touch, as cool as she longed to be. She had been so jittery all day about seeing Grant again. Her stomach twisted in knots at the idea of having to eat anything. How could she get through this night?

Take a deep breath. You can do it. You wanted a Christmas with friends, now you've got one.

Mr. Galloway, who had picked her up, smiled at her across the roof of the car. "Let's go inside. They're waiting for us."

Grant on the lookout for me. Emma's heart made a little jump. *Act normal. It's a family thing. Not a date.*

She followed Galloway up the steps and into the house. The smell of pine on the air was more pronounced than last time, though mixed with spicy scents from things cooking in the kitchen.

The heat enveloped her, and she shrugged out of her coat right away. Galloway took it from her and hung it on the rack.

Fay waved at her from the doorway into the kitchen. Bob at the hearth lifted a hand in greeting and then returned to his newspaper. Casey scrambled to get up from her place on the floor where she was doing a giant puzzle and ran to greet her. "What's in that bag? Is it a present?"

Emma leaned down. "Yes, for your grandma. She shouldn't see it yet. Where can I put it?"

Casey scanned the room. "Behind the sofa?"

"Great idea. You put it there. Careful, it's heavy."

Holding the bag with both hands, Casey carried it to the sofa.

Emma focused on her, ignoring the whispered question inside her. *Where is Grant?*

Did he take a job over the holidays, like last year?

Casey came back to her. "Done." She grabbed her hand and pulled her along. "You have to see this. Daddy cut a tree, especially for the both of us. Look at it. Isn't it pretty?"

The tree was about the perfect size for a little girl. There were golden bows, a heart with frosted snow on top, birds in different colors and sizes scattered across the branches. Some of them had long feathery tails, others had sequins on their chest, reflecting the light of the colorful little lamps blinking. There were even small presents underneath, in silver and golden paper with tags attached.

"You should have been here to decorate it with us," Casey said. "You shouldn't work so hard. Daddy said you can't help it that you have so many orders because your chocolate is so good, but I did think you could have left for an hour when Daddy asked you to."

She put her hands behind her back and pouted at Emma, all hurt indignation.

Emma blinked. *What is she talking about?* "Daddy asked me to?"

"Yes, he went into town to mail Christmas cards and he

asked you to come help us with the tree, but you were too busy." Casey kept a stern expression as if she wanted to drill the terribleness of that decision into Emma, then brightened in spite of herself. She stood on tiptoe and whispered as if it was a big secret, "I saved you something, though. You can put that in."

He hasn't been to the shop since the fair. Why would he lie to Casey?

The little girl ran to a bookcase and extracted something wrapped in pale pink tissue paper. She handled it as if it was extremely breakable.

Emma tried to wonder what it was, but her thoughts struggled with Grant's behavior. Maybe he'd glanced in and seen a crowd. The shop had been packed the last few days, also with family and friends of locals who had already flown in for Christmas and wanted to sample the local treats.

The shop closes at six. I could've gone after work.

Casey darted back to her and handed her the tissue-wrapped object. "Careful, it's easy to break."

"Okay." Emma sat down on a stool and leaned the object in her lap, peeling the fragile tissue paper away. It revealed a small glass donkey with the sweetest long ears.

"Daddy bought it for me on a trip. I love it so much. You can put it in the tree."

Emma swallowed hard. Casey wanted her to be a part of this, but, maybe, her dad didn't.

Just fake a headache and leave.

She couldn't bear to stay, thinking Grant didn't want her here. Her throat clogged, and her fingers trembled. *He's onto me. He wants to put some space between us. I could just melt into a puddle.*

She swallowed hard, driving her heels against the floorboards. *Casey wants you to be a part of it. And Mrs. Galloway has probably been working on dinner for hours.*

You're not leaving. Just play it cool.

She reached out to attach the donkey to a branch, close to a yellow light in the string, so the donkey's glass body started to twinkle with a warm glow.

Casey whooped and hugged her. "Now it's even better." She took a step back and looked at the tree. "Team Eagle's tree."

No. Emma's heart squeezed. *I'm not part of Team Eagle. He didn't want me here to help decorate.*

Casey pulled her to the table and pointed out that they all had star-shaped name cards indicating where they had to sit. "Fay says it's like a party. I love parties."

Emma wasn't looking for her own name, but for Grant's. When she spotted it, she almost exhaled in relief that he was here instead of having run off abroad.

Why are you so happy? He's the one who doesn't want you here.

The stairs creaked, and Grant came down. He had dressed up in a crisp white shirt and black pants. A black tie and gold cuff links gave his outfit class while the absence of a jacket underlined his casual style.

The moment their eyes met, they just stood and stared at each other. When he did start to move again, almost brusquely, he acted like he didn't know what to do or where to look.

Her heart skipped a beat. *Maybe he's as confused as I am, about what we are to each other.*

Casey pulled at her hand. "When are you going to give Grandma the surprise?"

"After dinner. First you tell me some more about this special tree. Did the birds also come from abroad?"

• • •

Grant had stayed upstairs too long pretending to have important phone calls, much to his mother's annoyance. It was a holiday after all, and what on earth could a person have to call people about on Christmas Eve?

But he had needed the time to pace the room and rehearse. To tell himself that once he came down, he would act normally around Emma. Not do anything on the forbidden list. Such as staring, moving closer to her, hoping she'd talk to him. He'd treat her like a friend. Period. But the moment he had walked down and seen her—the list burned to ashes.

He *was* already staring. He wanted to rush over and put his arm around her and tell her what he should have told her right after he had bought the charm. *I need you.*

He turned away abruptly and asked Bob something, then ambled to the table and studied the place cards. Good. Fay had not placed him beside Emma.

But he was opposite her.

Grant hesitated a moment, assessing whether that was good or bad. Looking her straight in the face, seeing her laughter, the sparkle in her eyes. He'd have to focus on the food on his plate all evening. Pretend it was so delicious he couldn't take his eyes off it.

"Ready for appetizers," his mother called. She and Fay carried out two large trays, one filled with small glasses with a reddish liquid in it and a breadstick laid out across, the other with half eggs filled with some sort of mousse. His father looked at it with disdain, as he wasn't a fan of fancy food as he called it. He'd rather have stew or even pancakes, regardless of the date on the calendar. Grant suppressed a grin and accepted a glass. "I suppose it's gazpacho?" He tried a sip. "Nice and spicy."

His mother shook her head at him as if she didn't take his compliment seriously. Or was it a silent reproach for having stayed up so long, almost running late for the start of their family dinner?

He whispered in her ear, "It's true. Your gazpacho is better than any I've had anywhere in the world." He was home. At last.

Emma also had gazpacho, dipping her breadstick into it. There was a hint of darkness under her eyes. Like she hadn't slept at all.

Someone has to watch over her and make sure she doesn't burn out.

He moved to stand beside her and asked in a low voice so the others wouldn't catch on, "Are you okay? Have you been working too hard?"

"No, I'm fine. Everything is fine. It was hectic but—it's over now." She twisted the breadstick around in her half full soup glass.

He nodded. Yes. *Rush hour is over. I don't have to help you with deliveries anymore. I can't make up excuses to come to the shop. It's over.* A void opened up inside of him, and the darkness outside the windows seemed to seep into the core of him. It was stupid because he had avoided the shop the last few days. Why couldn't he make up his mind?

"Wine, juice or water," his mother called and passed around the glasses. They were heavy crystal, kept for special occasions.

His father said, "Let's toast to family and the joy of Christmas."

They raised their glasses. "To the joy of Christmas."

Grant clinked his glass against Emma's. "To new beginnings."

Chapter Fifteen

New beginnings? Emma stared into Grant's chocolate eyes. *What does he mean? My new beginning in town? His new beginning in Florida? Or our...?*

No, there was nothing like "our." He lied to Casey that she couldn't come help with the tree. He didn't want her here.

But if he doesn't want me here, why is he looking at me like that?

She held her glass up, toasting the others, repeating well wishes without even knowing exactly what she was saying. *Don't let him confuse you. It doesn't mean anything special.*

A glass fell and broke. "Sorry." Fay stared down at the shards.

"I'll get a brush and dustpan," Mrs. Galloway said, bustling away into the kitchen.

Bob grabbed napkins off the table and dabbed at the liquid that ran across the floorboards.

Nobody is paying attention now. This is your chance. Emma said to Grant in a low voice, "Casey just showed me your tree. She had me add a last touch. She said I could have done it earlier, but you had told her I was too busy for it?"

Grant seemed taken aback. He held her gaze a moment, his expression shifting from surprise to concern. "Yes, I was… on my way when I changed my mind. I lied to Casey because she would be disappointed to hear you weren't coming. I'm sorry about that."

Uhm, that really doesn't explain anything.

She gave him a probing look. "You could have asked me and left the decision to me." She clenched her glass. His questions about her working too hard… "You seem to think I can't handle my business."

"I don't…"

Emma looked away. "Never mind." She didn't feel better arguing with him like that and besides, his family was all around them. This was a night meant for happiness and togetherness.

Grant caught her arm. His touch seemed to burn right through the fabric of her festive dress. "I'm really sorry."

Emma looked up into his eyes. The flash of hurt there took her off guard and she didn't know how to respond. "Did Casey make you put up the tree? Is it…connected with too many memories?"

Grant shook his head. "It was *my* idea. Casey asked about the golden bird and I found it in the attic. It was among all the things I took along when I sold the house in Chicago."

The house where they had lived as a family. "I see." On impulse she put her hand on his. "I'm sorry that it's been so hard for both of you."

Grant held her gaze. "That's not it. I realized when I was in the attic looking for the things my feelings about it have changed."

He seemed to want to say more, but his father's voice boomed, "So that's all cleaned up. Can we go to the table now? My stomach is grumbling."

Too bad. Emma pulled away from Grant and let Casey point out her place to her. She listened to the little girl chatter about what they'd be having, how the dessert was still a secret, but she already knew because she peeked in the fridge.

Mr. Galloway shook his head in mock reprimand, but he smiled. They were all smiling because Casey was happy.

All? Emma glanced at Fay and caught the tightness around her lips. *She must have dropped her glass because she's on the verge of tears. The bitter-sweetness of knowing it's the last time they'll be together like this.*

And Fay wasn't the only one. Soon Grant and Casey would be on the way to a life full of adventures. *Without me.*

If I could just hug him and tell him how much he means to me.

But not saying it was much easier. Pretending he was just a friend she'd let go. She was good at letting go. How different could it be this time?

If only she hadn't allowed herself to open up, to feel, to want. She had just had a taste of family life. And it wasn't nearly enough.

• • •

Casey had a bit of chocolate mousse on her cheek and a big grin on her face. His daughter was perfect. He was so proud of her and he loved her so much he couldn't even begin to comprehend it. The food and the wine filled his stomach with warmth, and outside the wind gently rattled at the windows, heaping more and more snow on the windowsills and covering everything with a layer of pure fluffy white. They were together, no need to go anywhere, or do anything. Just sit and enjoy.

"I'll read the story of Christmas now," his father said and got up to get the Bible and read from Luke about how the child had been born in Bethlehem and the shepherds had heard the angels sing.

Casey listened with wide eyes, her head tilted to the side.

Grant couldn't help looking at Emma as well. Was she angry? Her "you seem to think I can't handle my business" had punched him in the gut. How could he explain to her why he hadn't invited her over? *Yeah, uh, I realized that I like you just a little too much, so I walked away. That would really make it better. You can't explain. Not without creating even more hurt for her.*

His father asked them to join hands and pray. This time she wasn't holding his hand. He missed the warmth of her soft palm. How could he leave her behind?

"Amen," his father boomed.

Casey grinned at him, and Grant just knew she had some kind of plan.

Or had she just made a wish and expected it to come true on Christmas Eve?

His mother and Fay started to clean away the dishes while his father brought in more firewood which Bob piled onto the fire. Casey pulled Emma to the cupboard to look for board games. It was hot inside and it became even hotter with that fire being stoked.

Grant collected a few plates and carried them into the kitchen, but his mother waved him back into the living room, saying he had to make sure Casey didn't choose a board game she was too young for. "I don't want to see any tears because she can't play along with the grown-ups. Now scoot!"

Grant had a suspicious feeling she was steering him toward Emma. He ached for the carefree laughter they had once shared, before everything had become so complicated. And yet it had never not been complicated, because from day one he had known he was leaving. He had even told her. As if spelling it out would lay down some rules and then nothing could go wrong. *Think again.*

Casey put several colorful boxes with board games on the floor and was going over them, running her finger over the box and listing why it was fun or no fun. Emma sat on the low stool, watching her and chiming in every now and then with her opinion. She took care not to say that a game was too hard, but still weeded out those that weren't a good fit.

She's a natural with kids.

"So we could do this one and this one," Casey decided, picking up the boxes and clenching them to her chest. "They are perfect." She managed to scramble to her feet with her arms full and ran off to show her grandmother what she had come up with.

Emma sat up. Her expression turned distant, as if she was still present in the room, but not completely. He went over, not even knowing what pointless thing he could say. Something, anything to get a conversation started. Before he could reach her, she had jumped to her feet and headed to the fireplace. She leaned down as if she wanted to throw wood on the fire. "Let me do that." He came to her side, but she turned away and went into the kitchen. As if she were avoiding him.

I have to explain about the lie. He went after her, passing Casey, who came from the kitchen with his mother to lay out the board games on the cleared table.

He expected Fay to be in the kitchen but when he came in, only Emma was there at the sink, washing her hands. He could still hear the voices from the living room, talking, laughing, and still it seemed it was just the two of them here, in a world of their own.

A world in which it was very quiet as if everything was holding its breath waiting for him to do something, say the words he couldn't say.

She closed the tap and rubbed her hands with a towel. Her profile was outlined against the dark window behind her and he had never seen anything lovelier. How the hair fell to her shoulders and the way she held her head just a bit to the side as she was focusing on something. *Ask her how she feels about the two of you. If she's that special, you can't just let this slip by. You have to do something.*

His breathing rasped, and adrenaline raced through his system like during emergency proceedings on a plane. *Stick to the plan? Abandon it?* Those choices determined everything. The survival of everyone on board.

His little girl, their future. It had seemed all mapped out but now he was off track, feeling his way into new territory. Was he being selfish again, choosing his own happiness over what was best for his daughter? He didn't know. He couldn't think.

He shook his head and darted past Emma through the back door into the cold evening air. He inhaled the chill of the frost deep into his lungs to sober himself and restore that laser sharp focus he applied to his job in the air. Thoughts whirled like the snow, blinding him to the right direction to take. There were no beacons, nothing to navigate on.

It all comes down to trust.
Either you back off.
Or you jump in.

. . .

Grant's standing there like he wants to run away and never look back.

Emma's gut twisted. One moment he came for her and her breath caught hoping he would say something about them, the next he backed away and she was left deflated. This rollercoaster, up and down, a slow build, then a steep drop, could she take it much longer? *Let Casey give your present to Mrs. Galloway.* It would buy time and Grant could come back when he was ready. *He probably just needs a few minutes alone. Leave him be.*

But she didn't want to walk away. She wanted to be with him. Know what he was thinking even if it wasn't what she wanted to hear.

Starting your business, did you think you could do it? No. Dealing with difficult customers, handling a big event—I did it. All of it. I have to tell him how I feel. At least, try to.

She opened the back door. The jittering in her stomach swelled into a tornado. *Go on. He's worth it.*

She stepped outside.

The night air was crisp, but the wind had died down. It was perfectly still among the trees in the distance. She took a deep breath and relaxed her hands.

"It's okay whatever you're feeling right now. You're doing this big Christmas thing for Casey and she loves it." Her voice trembled a bit and she forced it to sound stronger. "Last year you were in a big city all alone and now you're here with your family and…maybe you think being alone was easier as you didn't have to pretend for anyone. But it's okay. Whatever you're feeling, it's okay."

She took another deep breath. "We can't force you to like Christmas. Maybe you would be happier flying right now. But you're here for Casey, and, like I said, I really think that's great. Also…" She had to clear her throat. "Your new job and all, setting up a place where you can raise her and…"

He turned to her in a whoosh. "You know about my new job?" His eyes were wide, almost startled.

Now he'll want to know how you found out about it. You can't give away Fay. Keep it vague.

"I heard about it."

"My family isn't happy." Tension lined his voice. "They want to keep me here."

"They can't. They must have known when you came here

it wouldn't be forever."

"Does that matter?" Grant laughed softly. "They feel like I'm leaving them behind."

So do I. Emma stared at her boots. Her eyes might give her away. *This is hard enough for him already. Don't show your disappointment.*

Grant moved closer to her. "What do you think?" His voice sounded urgent, needing reassurance. "Am I making a mistake?"

Say yes. This is your chance. He values your opinion. He said so before. That you always give him the right advice. Try and talk him out of it.

Her heart lit up a moment with the idea she could do this, change everything. All she had to do was point out some disadvantages to him, suggest it might not be the best thing for Casey's happiness. He would listen to her, believe her and… *Then hate you later for taking his dream job away from him, for a selfish reason? Not a chance.* "You should do it. If you believe it's the best thing for the both of you."

She took a deep breath to be able to go on. "It can't have been easy to find a job that fits the requirements you have to be able to raise Casey on your own. It's great you found something perfect."

Isn't it ironic? I'm applauding his choice, while I'm the last person in the world who wants to see him go. But I can't keep him here against his will.

"And I have never been to the Keys, but I heard it's beautiful there. Dolphins and whales and all the green on the islands. Especially if you can fly out with Casey, it must be amazing. Or go on a boat. I think she'll love that."

"She'll miss what she had here."

Her stomach shrank. He said "had" like it was already over.

There's really nothing left to discuss.

"But children adapt easily. Especially if their family is with them."

She faced him. "*You* are Casey's closest family, Grant. Not your parents, not Fay and Bob." *Not me, either.* "You. She needs you and as long as she has you, it's okay."

"Really?" He leaned closer to her. His eyes darkened. For one dazzling moment she was sure he was going to kiss her. It made no sense at all as she was saying all of this to let him go away from here, away from her, but there it was.

His face inched closer, his eyes were not just brown but had golden sparkles in them. Like the flame breaking to life in the lanterns on the Christmas fairground they had lit together. And she just knew there would be flames inside if he did kiss her.

"Grant? Oh, there you are." Fay's voice made them jerk apart. "Are you coming in? We've got the games all set up and snacks ready."

"Snacks?" Grant said. "I'm still stuffed from dinner." He passed her, brushing her hand with his, and it was like electricity flowed through her veins. *This doesn't change anything about the fact that he's leaving and you're staying.*

But it was Christmas. The time of year the impossible happened and wishes came true.

· · ·

"I won again!" Casey cried out and threw herself against Grant. He wrapped his arm around her and hugged her close. She rubbed her head across his shoulder and made a satisfied sound. Having his little munchkin with him was the best thing ever and he couldn't imagine anymore not being home for Christmas.

He glanced up at Emma on the other side of the table. She looked away to Bob, who wanted to refill her glass. *If I had kissed her, would she have liked it?*

Or smacked me in the face?

She was explaining it was okay to leave town. Go away from her. That doesn't add up with what I saw in her eyes.

But nothing added up anymore. He had believed he was climbing toward a new life and suddenly he had been in a completely different place, seeing another perspective. What would it be like to love again, and open his heart?

But Fay's intrusion had snatched the moment away, and maybe that was for the best. *Kissing her will make it so much harder than it already is. Feel what you want to but don't act on it.*

Emma nodded at Casey. "Time for the surprise."

Casey jumped to her feet. "It's Emma's surprise. I hid it." She ran to the sofa and pulled out a paper bag from behind it, holding it up. "Here it is." She carried it to his mother with both hands, then leaned against her to see what came out of the bag. A wrapped object. His mother looked at Emma. "You shouldn't have—"

She tore at the paper, revealing a teapot in the shape of a cupcake with pink frosting and a cherry on top forming the handle of the lid. Emma said, "I couldn't find anything chocolate related, so this seemed like a good alternative."

"It's gorgeous." His mother turned it around to look at it from all sides. Casey ran her finger across the frosting and pretended to lick it. "So sweet."

His mother put the teapot away and hugged Emma. "Thanks so much. It's a perfect addition to my collection." She held Emma by the shoulders and looked her over. "I found a great cupcake recipe we can try together."

Outside, a car engine hummed. Grant turned his head to listen. *Visitors, on Christmas Eve?* His father rose and moved away surreptitiously.

His mother gestured at Casey. "I think it's time for a

present for you."

"Me?" Casey perked up. "I thought I could only open them tomorrow morning." She sounded both confused and eager at her early chance.

His mother smiled. "We have something very special for you. Something you should see tonight."

Grant's father came back inside, carrying a twined basket in his arms. It was covered with a thin red blanket. A sound came from underneath. A sort of half-baked bark.

Grant's muscles tensed.

Dad, you haven't.

His father lowered the basket to the floor. The blanket moved. Casey's eyes were wide with disbelief. She leaned down and lifted the blanket. A small fluffy head popped up, black and white, with one ear tilted up and the other hanging. Casey squealed as she fell to her knees. "It's a puppy! It's a real puppy."

She put her hand into the basket and then looked up. "Is it for me?"

"Sure," his father said as if the arrival of a puppy had been a done deal. "Pick it up."

Grant frowned. How could Dad have done this without asking?

And Mom—why hadn't she stopped Dad?

He had a niggling suspicion they had done it on purpose to keep Casey and him here, where they could have family dinners and play games and raise this puppy. Together. But it wouldn't work. He had accepted a job offer, and he was leaving town. Every time he reiterated it, the conviction underneath dwindled, and especially now. *Just look at the two of them.*

Carefully, her tongue between her lips, Casey lifted the puppy out of the basket. He had icy blue eyes and a long pink tongue that licked at Casey's face. His daughter put the puppy on her shoulder, as if it was a baby. His throat constricted. He had once carried her like that. A little human being, safely tucked against him, in the crook of his arm. So small, so vulnerable, all his to protect. He'd do anything for her. Anything. Even let her keep the puppy who had wriggled its way into her heart so quickly. The smile on her face was the best Christmas gift he could imagine.

Or was there an even better one? Surrender to what he knew deep down inside was the only way to find happiness again. Shelter Emma in his arms, listen to her struggles with difficult customers and brush the worry lines from her face. Do fun things together and laugh until their sides hurt. Make memories they would cherish forever. *I need her and I love her. I want her to be a part of our family.*

Why be a team of two, if they could also be a team of four? Her, him, Casey, the puppy.

Everybody was fussing over that little dog. *Perfect.* He ran up the stairs. In his room, he fished the box with the Christmas tree charm from the drawer where he had buried it. All alarm bells were ringing in the back of his head. *This isn't smart, this isn't safe. Don't do it.*

With every step of the stairs, his heartrate increased. The box pricked in his palm. *All or nothing.* He gestured to Emma. She seemed confused, raising a brow, but as he mouthed "come with me" she walked over to him. He drew her into the kitchen. Everything faded, Casey's squealing, Dad's deep baritone.

This is it.

He clutched the box like a lifeline. "I have to ask you something."

• • •

Emma clenched her hands by her sides. "The puppy wasn't

my idea."

Grant blinked. Then he smiled. "I didn't want to ask about the puppy."

"Oh." A bit of tension slipped as she answered his smile. "I was worried you thought it was my idea."

"No, I can guess it was my parents' doing. Or Fay's. She can't say no to a cute dog. I recognized that face when I saw it. It's from friends of hers. Their dog had eight puppies a few weeks ago."

He took a deep breath. "So…"

Emma's stomach tightened. He seemed so serious. Was he gearing up for something? If it wasn't about the dog…

Grant said, "I realized—uh—"

He held out his hand. A present rested on his palm, in seasonal wrapping paper. "When I came to town to ask you to decorate Casey's tree with us, I bumped into a sign in the street, advertising Christmas presents. On impulse I decided to get you something."

"You shouldn't have."

"I bought it and then I…couldn't come over. Just because…"

She frowned. *What's going on?*

"See what it is." He held it out.

"Okay." She picked up the present and tore off the paper. Her fingers trembled. A box from a jewelry store. She clicked it open. A silver charm rested on a bit of blue velvet. A Christmas tree with white enamel snow on top.

"For your bracelet," he said softly. "Your first Christmas here in Wood Creek."

The first charm not bought by herself. A gift for her. A contribution to a project she had started alone. She touched the tree with her fingertip. "That's sweet." Her voice wobbled. How could she wear this every day, while he was far away from her?

"I had it wrapped for you and while waiting, I realized that...it wasn't just a gift I was buying for a friend. You've come to mean much more to me."

Emma flinched.

He feels something, but it can't be. He's leaving.

Ice filled her stomach as it had when her bags were being packed again. And she had waved goodbye through the rear window of the car, goodbye to another house, a family, a time of being together that had come to an end.

Don't do this to me, not now, not on the best Christmas Eve I've ever had.

"I understand. You have Florida." She couldn't get out more.

"I took the job in Florida and planned my life with Casey there, because I didn't want complications to..."

Complications. His feelings for her were just complications. Roadblocks to the future he had in mind. *Make it easy on him.*

"I'm sorry," she said softly. "You have to believe me when I say that as Casey asked me to make the chocolates to let you fall in love, I never meant to have you fall in love for real."

Grant eyed her. "What?" he asked as if he couldn't believe his ears.

"I mean, for you to fall in love with anyone. I just wanted to help Casey. She wanted to make you happy and that was just so sweet. I never meant for any of this—" Emma's hands trembled, and she clutched the box with the charm. "It just happened."

Grant kept his eyes on her face. "What happened?"

Give him an honest answer? What's the point? He made it clear he doesn't want to get entangled.

"I like you," she said.

A lopsided smile spread across his face.

"Just like me?"

Emma pressed her heels hard on the floor. "It's not something to tease me about."

"Of course not." His expression sobered. "I'm not teasing. Far from it."

Hurt flickered in his eyes. She reached out and put her hand on his arm. "I didn't mean to make this more difficult. I understand. We met at the wrong time. Had we met earlier, then we might have—but you're leaving. I—I am happy for you and Casey."

She swallowed. "You helped me so much with delivering my orders. Your whole family has been amazing. Me being here tonight is so special. Normally, I would just have been alone. I'm grateful." It would be a happy memory. She'd make it one.

Grant reached out and cupped her cheek in his palm. The warmth of his touch invaded her system and stopped her breath. "I don't want you to ever be alone again," he said.

Wait. What?

She frowned.

"When I realized I was falling in love with you, I backed away."

Falling in love? Her brain caught on the words and refused to process anything more.

"I had just gotten back on my feet and I didn't want to feel anything like that again. I had to protect myself and Casey. I tucked away the charm and pretended nothing had happened. I threw myself into getting everything ready for the move, to fight the bad feeling I had about leaving. But I was wrong." He took a deep breath. "I usually go for what I want, whether it's conquering a mountain or getting into an isolated place where only small planes can go. I like challenges. And I want to ask you if you're willing to accept this challenge with me. If you want to be with me."

What? Emma stared at him. This had to be a dream. *He*

can't be saying this.

"Be with you?" she repeated to make sure.

He nodded.

"But…" Her thoughts whirled. "I have the shop. I signed a lease for the building. I can't leave town for four years."

"I wouldn't ask you to leave town. I know how many times you had to move and give up everything you loved. Your business is here, and your friends are here. You're staying. We'll find a way."

She didn't see how. They couldn't afford to fly out to each other all the time. A long-distance relationship for four years?

He leaned in and kissed her. As his lips caressed hers, his arms slipped around her, securing her against him. She closed her eyes and soaked up the tenderness of his touch, the reassurance he was here for her.

Even if they couldn't see each other often, they'd make the most of the times when they could. She had something here, in his arms, which she would never have had in the shop alone or with the chocolate creations. This was life at its sweetest and it was all hers.

Grant lifted his head and looked at her. "I should have done this sooner," he said, slightly breathless.

Emma grinned at him. "I wouldn't have minded."

He kissed her again and she reached up and put her hand on his head, burying her fingers in his hair. She let her hand run down his neck to rest on his shoulder, not quite able yet to take in this gorgeous man was now hers.

"You're kissing!" a voice yelled, and they broke apart.

Casey was staring at them from the doorway. "You were kissing," she said in an almost accusing tone. "Daddy, you said you didn't like kissing."

Emma didn't dare look at Grant to see how he was going to talk himself out of this one. But before he could speak,

Casey said, "I know why you like it now. It was the chocolate. I wanted the chocolate to help and it did."

She ran over to Emma and looked up at her. "You're much better than Miss Evelyn. You helped me to sing." She beamed again at the memory. "I was so scared, but you said I could do it."

Emma brushed her hand across Casey's head. "I'll help you with anything you want me to. You can count on it."

Casey locked her arms around Grant's waist. "I can keep the puppy, right? Please? He's so sweet."

Grant crouched to look her in the eye. "Who's going to take care of him?"

"I am."

"But you will be in school again."

"Grandpa can or Grandma or Fay or Bob. Someone."

"But if Daddy finds a job away from here, they won't be there. What will we do with the puppy while you're at school?"

"Then I want to stay here." Casey crossed her arms over her chest. "You go flying alone."

"All alone?" Grant made an exaggerated face of surprise. "You're not coming with me?"

"Not if I can't bring Puppy." Casey nodded. "You can fly here too. You don't need to go away."

Emma watched the two of them, her heart pounding. It was a child's response of course, but she could sympathize.

"You're right, Casey. I can fly here too. I could look into jobs and…" He rose to his feet and eyed Emma. "I could stay around here. How about that?"

Emma stared at him. "But you wanted to go and—"

Grant shook his head. "Casey is right. I'll need to find a job that leaves me time to raise her, an unruly puppy and… see a whole lot of you." He leaned over and brushed a kiss on her temple. Her heart skipped and she wanted to throw up her arms and whoop. This was just perfect.

Casey ran off, shouting that Daddy was staying and they would all be together with Emma.

"What about Florida?" Emma whispered.

"We'll go there someday. On holiday. I can't wait to show you everything from the air." Grant wrapped his arm around her shoulders. "But there's no way I'm moving so far away from you. Not for a job, not for anything."

She leaned into him as he led her into the living room.

Four pairs of eyes were watching her expectantly. Bob seemed puzzled, but Fay beamed and exchanged a quick look with her mother.

"Welcome to the family." Mr. Galloway rose and came for her with an outstretched hand. "We're so happy to have you."

"Thanks so much." Emma shook his hand, her throat tight a moment. "This means the world to me."

Casey scooped up Puppy and held him in her arms as she stood in front of the big Christmas tree. The hundreds of glittering lights illuminated her with a fairytale quality, putting an extra sparkle in her eyes.

Grant smiled down at his daughter, and Emma locked her arms around him and drank in the sight of her little family.

A family by Christmas was the best gift of all.

Acknowledgments

Thanks to all the authors, editors, and agents who share online about the writing and publishing process.

Special thanks to everyone who works with me on the Little Shops on Heart Street series: my amazing agent Jill Marsal; the entire dedicated team at Entangled, especially Candace, Liz, Heather, and Curtis; and last but certainly not least, cover designer Bree Archer for the festive cover.

The idea for the little shops was born from my own love of shopping in small, family-owned businesses and, in that way, supporting people's dreams. These businesses often carry unique products and show attention to detail in every aspect, from the shop decorations to the expert advice. I loved creating fictional Wood Creek and its artisan shops on Heart Street, especially the cute chocolate shop and all the sweet treats Emma puts together. From the moment I pictured this snow-drizzled girl entering the chocolate shop with her special request, the story took off. I included some of my own wintery favorites—building snow dogs and visiting a Christmas fair full of sparkly booths, festive music and great food—and hope that all this seasonal cheer brings a smile to your face and the hope to your heart that, no matter what happens in life, good things are just around the corner.

Please return to Wood Creek for *A Valentine's Proposal*, in which bookshop employee Cleo Davis agrees to a daring wager with the shop's new owner to stop him from changing everything about it, but falling in love with her boss may prove to be the greatest challenge of all. Happy reading!

About the Author

With the same trademark atmospheric settings, relatable characters and cute canines that made several of her cozy mysteries #1 Amazon US and Canada bestsellers in multiple categories, Vivian Conroy pens romance as Viv Royce, creating the little shops on Heart Street she herself would like to frequent to stock up on bonbons, books and cute home decorations. When not hanging out in fictional worlds, she likes to hike, craft and spend too much time on Twitter where readers can connect via @VivWrites.

Find your Bliss with these great releases...

THE DADDY COACH
a novel by Karen Muir

Instant fatherhood hits contractor Will Sinclair hard when his twin sons he didn't know existed come to live with him. The rebellious boys reject Will as their real dad, forcing him to turn to Gina, his new nanny, for her "expert" help. Interacting with Will and his boys as a "daddy" coach, Gina starts to crave the family she's always longed to have. But Will's reaction when he learns of her deception isn't her biggest fear––one of two men she loves is lying...

THE SOCCER PLAYER AND THE SINGLE MOM
a novel by Kyra Jacobs

The last thing soccer player Scott Gillie wants or needs is a persistent and entirely too distracting PA while he's recuperating in his small hometown. Unfortunately, it's not up to him. Then Felicity and her son end up temporarily moving in—all thanks to his meddlesome grandmother. Now temptation is right across the hall and it's driving Scott crazy. His only option is to fight fire with fire. He never expects Felicity to do the same.

Catching Her Heart
a *For the Love of the Game* novel by Jody Holford

Sure, Addison Carlyle may have kinda maybe kidnapped one of her professional baseball players, but it's for a *really* good cause. She desperately needs someone high-profile to auction off for the multiple sclerosis society she's chairing, but Sawyer McBain insists he wants a favor in return. Soon Addie and Sawyer are trading completely ridiculous I.O.U.s, like being his plus-one to his grandmother's poker game or keeping each other company at the driving range. But when their agreement goes from flirty to fiery, neither is ready to let their guard down for a shot at love.

Unexpectedly Yours
a novel by Coleen Kwan

Derek Carmichael has harbored a secret crush on his best friend's older sister for years, but Hannah has always been out of his reach. Hannah is wary of Derek's player past and the rampant rumors connecting him to beautiful socialites. Still, she can't help but give in when their attraction reaches a boiling point. Trying to keep it a secret from her overprotective brother is one thing, but when Hannah finds herself unexpectedly expecting, her life is thrown upside down. She and Derek may be becoming parents together, but that's no basis for a happily-ever-after.

9 781694 079374